prologue

It begins with a boy.

It begins with a boy and it ends with a boy, but what story doesn't?

In my eyes, this one is the most amazing person I've ever met. And maybe some people would say that I loved him too much and forgot myself in the process, but from what I've seen of relationships, there's always that one person who does.

Last night, my world that had been so small and wrapped up in everything about him, came to a grinding halt. I can't sleep. I need to do *something*. I've decided to write it out from beginning to end. How we arrived at this place.

This is my story. Our story.

It's about an incredible guy who changed my mind about everything I thought I knew. And maybe I helped change his world, too.

So here it is.

This isn't your run-of-the-mill fairy tale. It's not some Harlequin romance. I wouldn't even categorize this as much of a romance at all.

Because I'm not the kind of person to fall in love.

And neither is the guy I'm head over heels for.

I'm Lilly Grace Evans and this is the true account of how I ended up falling for a boy who made me believe love is anything but conventional.

Love, for those lucky enough to experience it, is extraordinary.

Amber L. Johnson

chapter
one

I wasn't supposed to meet him.

My best friend, Harper, had been told she could no longer babysit for Wednesday Night Prayer Meetings because she'd been stupid enough to put a three year old on a window sill – ("It was CLOSED!") – The poor toddler leaned against the screen until it popped out, sending him tilting out the window and almost to his death.

This is quite unacceptable anywhere, but God help you if it happens in Allentown, Pennsylvania.

Luckily, he was okay, but our pastor got involved and suggested maybe she wasn't the best fit for the job. That's how I got asked to take her place. I'd shown up at the Neely house, and while my mom dropped off a crockpot of meatballs, I was pointed towards a bonus room holding exactly one other occupant: a boy.

It was the first time I met Colton Neely. Nine years old. Dark brown bowl cut hair and eyes that strayed everywhere but on me. The room was filled to the brim with coloring books, art pads, and paints. And trains. Oh my God, don't get me started on the trains . . . bins of them in every corner.

He wanted to color for the two hours I was with him. At the time, I barely thought anything of being paid to sit with a boy so close to my age while our parents were in the next room – I was getting *paid*, after all. Halfway through the first picture in his coloring book, that he refused to share with me by the way, I looked over and gently grabbed hold of his hand to stop him from what he was doing.

"You need to color inside the lines. That's what they're for." I admonished him with the brazen bitchiness only a ten year old girl with a superiority complex could muster.

See, I believed you could tell a lot about a person by the way they color.

I used to think there were two kinds of Crayola artists: Ones who color inside the lines and ones who don't stay within the rigid boundaries set by thick black perimeters that make up a cuddly koala.

But it seems that inside and outside the lines is just the main basis for comparison. You also have those who color lightly inside and fill each space according to the chosen and appropriate shade.

Then you have those who scribble and slap any color anywhere. And sometimes these people have purple turkeys and shit that drives me absofreakinglutely crazy because, seriously . . . *who has purple turkeys?*

Then you have people who take the time to outline each portion of the picture with color before filling it in, so it not only looks cohesive, but it seems like they actually give a damn about the big-eyed My Little Pony they're giving definition to.

Or, you have those who make little polka dots in the middle of a bear's face and then cry excitedly that the bear has chicken pox.

See where I'm going with this? Society has pretty much taught us that it's inside the lines, or outside. But there's so much more in between.

I wanted to correct Colton so he'd be like everyone else.

He didn't even look up from the paper, but flinched and quickly pulled his hand away from mine. "You're mean," he whispered and continued to make sweeping motions across the paper, coloring in wide strokes of every vibrant hue he could get his little fingers on. It was the first words he'd spoken to me, and they would reverberate through my brain for years to come.

Was I mean?

I don't like people being mad at me, or not liking me, so I tried to make up for it.

"Wanna go outside?" I'd asked, afraid he'd tell my mom I'd hurt his feelings.

"It's raining." He'd said it so matter-of-fact, like he was the adult and I was some stupid little kid.

Colton was not going to get the best of me, you see. I was going to make $15 that day. And I was going to get this kid to give a good report to his mother.

"It's not raining that bad."

"My mom says I'm not allowed."

"No one will notice. Come on. Let's go outside."

It was the first time I'd get him to do something he wasn't too sure of. We'd gone out into the rain on that balmy summer day. He'd looked into the sky with wide, pale blue eyes that appeared much too mature for his age, and he'd simply muttered something about the chances of getting hit by lightning.

I didn't really pay attention, though. He had a badass swing set with a sandbox in his back yard and I was too busy trying to get up the slide from the front, instead of taking the ladder, because I wanted to be one of those chicks on television who kicked ass. And my first step would be to get up a slide. In the rain.

It's called 'preparation'.

Colton had run over to me, his hands waving up and down at his sides frantically as I huffed and puffed my way up the slick metal. "You'll get hurt!"

I'd rolled my eyes and shushed him. "I'm fine."

That's when the first lightning bolt hit the tree a few feet away from the slide I was struggling to get up.

Poor little Colton covered his ears and jumped about a foot into the air.

I had watched in awestruck wonder as he'd turned around ridiculously fast and sprinted across the backyard, screaming as his legs propelled him forward while he leaped over puddles of water two feet wide to get back to the house.

Leaving me on the metal slide.

Alone.

Where I *did* get hit by lightning.

Well, not me. The slide. The slide got hit by lightning and I was holding on to it so I sort of just spazzed out and my arm hair was standing on end by the time I shook hard enough to get my fingers to let go of the side of the slide. Then I fell back into the mud and blacked out.

When I woke up in the hospital, my mom informed me Colton had been freaking out and his mom finally got enough information out of him so that *my* mom could pull me across the lawn and into the house. Both of them were hysterical. And I was lucky to be alive.

He had essentially saved my life.

Then he showed up at the hospital with his mom, Sheila, looking at me like I was the most fascinating thing in the world because I *wouldn't die*.

I did get this amazing scar from the experience, though. My doctor said it was called a Lichtenberg Figure, this crazy raised skin that was darker than the rest of my complexion. It looked like tree roots running from the top of my shoulder to the middle of my arm. I was enamored with it at the time.

Apparently Colton was, too.

Now it's just a thing on my body. Part of who I am. Sometimes I forget it's there.

Back to the story.

He stayed for a good thirty minutes, not speaking and not doing anything other than staring at me – at my new battle wound that I hoped portrayed I actually *was* a badass. Right before he left, he pulled a folded piece of paper out of his pocket and handed it over, offering me a small wave before walking out behind his mother.

That piece of paper held the most intricately colored artwork I'd ever seen in my life.

Instead of making me feel better, it made me feel bad.

Because just the day before, I had apparently told The Artist of our Generation to color inside the effing lines.

* * *

I met Colton under the guise that I was getting paid to sit for some kids from church. But every time I showed up to the house, it was just us two.

I had to wonder why I was getting paid to hang out with him in the first place. I mean, *really*?

You would think after I almost died I wouldn't be asked to come over anymore. But you'd be wrong because apparently his mom didn't learn a lesson once. I'm sure it was because she felt like her son was good enough that we wouldn't get into trouble, but she didn't take into account that *I* wasn't.

Colton's pretty much perfect. He's quiet and aloof, always minds his manners and whatnot. As a child, he was continuously focused on coloring or drawing or even painting in the room his dad had cleaned out above the garage.

I didn't want to paint or make boy-trains. I got tired of coloring.

I just wanted to play, ya know?

Needless to say, he probably stopped trusting me a whole lot the day I almost choked on a marble. And the time I accidentally got gum stuck in my hair and asked him to help me cut it out. Which resulted in a huge chunk of hair missing on the left side of my head.

His trust of me must have taken a nosedive the day I tried to teach him how to mattress surf down the stairs, but since he was being so adamant about not participating, I decided to show him exactly how much fun it could be. I got onto the mattress backward, staring him in the face as I pushed off the top stair and started to head backward down the stairwell. Except . . . the mattress didn't come with me.

Not at first, anyway.

I rolled onto my back and went head first into the corner next to the front door and hit my head so hard it gave me a concussion. Colton had to push the mattress off me because it was only five seconds delayed behind my limp body. And then he started screaming for our moms and they called another ambulance while they freaked out. I threw up green hot dogs or something crazy on the way to the hospital. Once I was coherent enough to speak to her behind the flimsy blue curtain in the ER, I assured my mom it was my fault.

Funny enough, she believed me.

That time, when Colton and his mother came to see me in the hospital, it was to announce I was no longer going to be invited over on Wednesday nights. And they were changing churches.

It took all of *that* for her to realize I was incapable of keeping myself out of harm's way. Amazing.

Anyway, Colton had stayed even more quiet than usual, and he'd barely looked at me the entire time he was there. But before he left, he'd given me another picture. And let me tell you, this one was even more beautiful than the one before because it was a page full of nothing but color.

He'd scratched at his hair hidden beneath his favorite baseball cap and whispered, "Bye, Lilly." I'd given him a final wave, knowing deep in my heart it was probably going to be the last time I would see him for a very long time.

I was pretty much right. Mrs. Neely had been talking to my mother out of what she assumed was earshot, but I could still hear what was going on. At the time, her words didn't make much sense. Although, they do now.

Because it took me another five years to figure out exactly what was so different about Colton Neely and why his mother was so upset that she couldn't find a playmate for him.

7

Amber L. Johnson

chapter two

When I was younger, I always thought everyone was the same. So it didn't really faze me all that much that Colton kind of just faded away. He was someone I hung out with for a few weeks and then he just . . . wasn't. He became another kid I once knew.

A few years passed and I didn't think about him anymore. Harper and I moved on from playing like tomboys to paying attention *to* boys. She would flirt and I would laugh at how obvious she was. But beneath it all, I really wished I had her kind of confidence, which I sincerely lacked.

It wasn't until my parents forced me to go on a camping trip that I realized I was capable of getting the attention of boys, too.

It turns out I didn't like it much.

I'd fought them tooth and nail; because I just wanted to stay home and read books or watch television, or hang out with Harper or anything else other than spend time with my family. I'd sulked the entire way there, my earbuds in and a scowl on my face, annoyed I wasn't an adult and able to make my own decisions.

While they went and took nature walks, I wandered over to the beach with a book in hand and my headphones, hell bent on getting some sort of tan because I was practically translucent. But instead, I met a boy named Rory. He was splashing in the water, clearly having a good time with what turned out to be his younger sister. She was less than impressed and whining about being in the water, but I couldn't help notice how cute it was that they were playing together.

Apparently, I caught Rory's eye because he kept staring at me. At first, I figured it was my scar, as I'd grown increasingly self-conscious about it as I got older. But he wasn't looking at that. He was watching me like a stalker.

You know what I mean. That kind of uncomfy stare that makes you shift around and turn in random directions to make sure there isn't some freakishly good looking supermodel sitting behind you grabbing a male's attention. I kept moving around on my beach towel, convinced this cute, tan boy with shaggy brown hair wasn't staring at me. But he totally was.

Eventually it got hot and I waded out into the water, only to be hit by a spray of wetness coming from the pissed little sister of said cute boy whose gaze I was half-heartedly avoiding.

"Penny, apologize to her." He'd pointed in my direction and I froze because he was actually paying attention to me and it caught me off guard.

I waved my hand and shook my head. "It's okay."

He waded over and smiled, running his hands through his hair and it was then I realized he had these really light green eyes. I had never seen anything like it in my young teenage life. They were breathtakingly clear, and with his tan, they stood out even more. It may have been the first time I ever felt my heart flutter, but there was also a weird sort of reaction in my stomach that felt a lot like queasiness.

He introduced himself and we spent the next couple hours ignoring Penny and talking in the water. Then, right before it was time to head back to my tent, we walked over to my beach towel and I realized sweet Rory . . . was sporting a raging boner.

In his swimming trunks.

It was pointing directly at me and I swear to the good Lord in heaven above it scared the shit out of me. I couldn't help but stare at it with wide eyes and an open mouth, trying not to point.

Instead, I packed my stuff in a hurry and rushed back to the safety of my tent and wondered if all guys were like that. If I was doomed to a life of uncontrollable hard-ons and pretty boys with light green eyes who pointed their sticks at me with wild abandon.

Rory eventually found me in the campground and tried to hang out a couple more times, but I always made an excuse to not be anywhere around him. I even went so far as to spend time with my dad.

He handed me a note the last day we were there, giving me his phone number and asking me to call him. Asking me to be his girlfriend.

But it wasn't right.

That's the way it went for the next two years. I met a lot of guys who I thought were nice enough, but they never sparked anything other than platonic interest from me. I focused on being friends with guys, helping Harper get her fill of attention from willing participants in her kissing games. I just didn't care. Boys were fun, but they were more fun to hang out with. And yet, I constantly felt like there was some sort of unexplainable void inside me.

Something was missing.

You know that feeling like you forgot something? When you pack for a trip and it's not until you're on the plane that you realize you left one of your most important possessions, like your iPhone, back at the house? Yeah, you do. I carried that feeling around with me for years. *Years*.

Then, during the summer I turned fifteen, I found what I'd been looking for.

One afternoon, my mom dropped me and Harper off at this weird little craft fair held in the next county over. I was just psyched to get to eat funnel cakes. She, on the other hand, was on the prowl for cute boys. We wandered through some of the exhibits, and while I was more interested in the cool stuff people were creative enough to make, she wasn't.

Her long blond hair was pulled up in a ponytail and she'd purposely worn this denim skirt that pretty much showed her underwear that my mom had tskd at in the car ride over. She was working on a sucker like she'd been paid to do candy-porn and was as bored as I'd ever seen her. Her blue eyes were rolling as she turned the corner in a tent full of Native American jewelry.

"Let's go. Call your mom to pick us up. This suuuuucks."

I laughed and shook my head, letting go of the tissue paper flower I'd been studying. "We just got here."

"And I'm already bored."

"Fine." I turned to lead her toward the exit when I saw a crowd of people surrounding one of the exhibits. It was brightly colored and there was artwork hanging everywhere in and around the tent. Suddenly, I wasn't so interested in leaving. Because right smack-dab in the middle of the crowd was none other than Colton Neely.

He'd grown up considerably. His hair had turned much darker than the last time I had seen him, but I recognized his eyes, even from several feet away.

They put Rory's to shame.

I was sucked into this weird-ass vortex where I couldn't take my eyes off him, but was too scared to approach because what if he didn't recognize me?

Trying to play it cool, I slipped through the crowd and pretended to be interested in the artwork hanging in and around his tent. It was impressive enough to warrant my attention, don't get me wrong, but just being within ten feet of him made my fifteen year old hormones shoot straight through the roof. From the conspicuous side-eye I was giving him, I could see he was so much more attractive than the little boy who'd saved my life all those years ago. He was taller and leaner, almost too thin. It made my heart hurt to be so close and not speak to him.

Harper finally found a guy to talk to and I was thankful for her sudden departure so I could walk around Colton's exhibit. It was beautiful and I couldn't help but smile as I passed some of his paintings.

And then . . . like crazy radar in my brain, I stood in front of one spectacular piece, just floored by how gorgeous it was. Thick lines of paint covering every last inch of canvas, running together to create new colors and hues I'd never seen before. I just stared, my mouth probably open in an embarrassing look of quiet disbelief.

That's when I heard him speak next to my ear. "Lilly?"

I have to admit, the sound of his voice made my insides nosedive like an unsteady paper plane. I turned around and gazed into his face and smiled. Probably way too big. "Hey, Colton."

God. Do you have any idea what was going on inside my body? It was like Christmas lights dropped in a puddle of water. I felt electrocuted by his gaze. Those eyes, still so trusting, still so observant, raked over my face just to stare silently.

"These are awesome." I tried to compliment him. But he didn't seem to be affected by my praise. "Are you selling them?"

Yes, stupid question. I was young and intimidated by a cute boy.

"Yes."

"Cool."

Ah, yes. I always was a conversationalist at heart.

It was about that time Mrs. Neely called and waved him over to a potential buyer and I was left standing like an idiot, trying not to lean against anything and take the entire tent down with me in the process. At just the moment I had decided to leave, he suddenly appeared by my side again, his face scrunched.

Puddle Jumping

"Would you like to go for a walk?"

Like I would say no. My brain was completely fried in front of him.

We snuck around behind the back of the tent and between the other vendors until we'd reached the edge of the woods. About fifty feet away were the train tracks that ran through the area. I'd never paid much attention to them before, but after that day, the sound of a train whistle would always remind me of that day.

"How have you been?" I asked, looking at the trees around me instead of at him because I felt suddenly really insecure.

He was quiet and I stopped walking, turning back to see where he was because he wasn't by my side. He was kneeling down, face to face with a tiny patch of flowers. I walked back over and knelt down next to him, checking out the clump of weeds.

Colton silently focused on them before finally, *finally* turning to gaze at my lips. "Did you know your name means 'beautiful'?" My mouth must have fallen open because my tongue instantly went dry and I couldn't form words. He just looked back down at the plant and whispered, "Beautiful grace. I looked it up."

His stare averted so quickly, it made my cheeks burn bright red and my hands go sweaty.

He'd inadvertently told me I was beautiful.

And I kinda believed him.

Despite the scar on my arm I'd been teased about for years that made me feel like a freak.

Despite the fact that I wasn't as pretty as my best friend.

I like to remember that moment at the fair. How I felt that day.

Colton was just so quiet and we didn't talk much, though he stared and watched me for what felt like forever.

Eventually, I couldn't take the awkward silence anymore. "So, you're a big famous artist, huh?"

I just remember vividly how damn sweaty my hands were at the time.

Colton stopped walking and was staring into the trees, his hands shoved deep into his pockets while he gazed above our heads. I wanted to touch him or just be close enough to him to feel his arm brush against mine, but was so freaking nervous about it all I couldn't form a coherent sentence to save my life. For a second he looked like he was going to reach out

13

and touch my arm, but as quickly as his hand lifted, it went right back to his side.

That was essentially all the time we had together before a short train came roaring by and Colton covered his ears like he had all those years ago in the rain. His eyes were squeezed shut and when it passed, I could hear his mother calling for him. Frantically. He dropped his hands and walked in her direction as if it was what he was expected to do. I fell back, my feelings hurt that he would just run away from me at the first chance he'd gotten.

Because it was all about me, after all.

When I cleared the trees, I worked my way back to his tent, my hands yanking on the hem of my shirt and my brain screaming that if I was someone pretty, like my best friend, then maybe he wouldn't have abandoned me back there.

Harper was a little off to the side from where I had left her and she was definitely making out with the guy she'd made her moves on before I'd taken a walk. He was skinny and tall and his pants were halfway down his ass while his hand was halfway up her skirt. She was kissing him in that sloppy way that makes me throw up in my mouth a little.

I cleared my throat and she pulled the lower half of her face out of his unhinged jaws long enough to smile and pop a bubble with the pink gum from the center of her sucker.

"You ready to go?" I asked, trying to only look at her and not back at the tent.

Since it wouldn't have been obvious to anyone within a five foot radius that I was looking every damn place except the huge tent of pretty paintings set up directly to my left.

It would have been funny, what with the way I was looking toward it but then above and around until I was sure my eyes had cleared the top so they could land just on the other side. Except, I was trying not to cry.

Harper introduced me to her new suck-face partner, Clay. And with as much as I didn't like him then, I'm thankful for him now. Because he had some information I'd been missing.

Clay looked me over and must have noticed me purposely not looking at Colton's tent. His stare moved from me to it at least a half dozen times before he licked his lips and nodded toward the art on display.

"Can you believe this kid?"

I started to look over my shoulder but stopped in time before I made that fatal mistake.

"Who?" Harper asked.

Puddle Jumping

Clay pointed and I wanted to punch him in his junk because now it would be super obvious if I didn't follow his movement. So we all turned and looked toward the tent and I bit my tongue to stop from saying something stupid.

"The Neely kid does these crazy paintings that are selling for major cash."

Harper's eyes went wider than I'd ever seen them before as she turned to face me. "The kid who saved your life? Colton, right?"

He nodded. "Yeah. He's some kind of art whiz."

"What does that mean?" I asked, not because I was an idiot, but because he was being weird about it.

Clay gave me some stupid look that made me want to shove him in the top of the spin-art machine and watch his head whirl around and around and around . . .

What? You watched late night movies on HBO with the sound down so your parents didn't know. Don't lie.

"It means he's a genius with paint or something." Clay's eye rolling just added to my mental horror movie.

"Geniuses are smart, right?" Harper was playing up the dumb blonde bimbo for this moron. I mean, come on . . .

"Yeah. Smart. He's also 'special.' " He held his fingers in air quotes.

"Special . . . like . . ." I was so not following the conversation, you know? "Didn't your mom ever tell you that you were special? Mine does."

"Special like he's not normal." Harper answered for him.

"You're not normal. Who *is* normal?"

Who cared if Colton was? He was golden in my book.

"He's autistic."

But I heard 'artistic' and gave him a 'No. Really?' look. "Of course he's artistic. He sells art."

Clay huffed in annoyance and sprinted toward the tent. My entire body flushed hot as I saw him grab a flyer from one of the tables before slipping back through the crowd to hand it to me.

It was the very first time I'd ever heard of Asperger's.

15

Amber L. Johnson

chapter three

Colton has Asperger's.

Asperger's.

Say it a million times over.

It's such a foreign word, right? And I'm sure there's a hell of a lot of people that know about this stuff from the get-go, but I wasn't one of them. It's not like, at the age of fifteen and in the midst of my daily gossip sessions with Harper, we'd suddenly stop to wax philosophic over the different types of Autism and spectrum disorders in the world.

We were more into talking about Fashion Police and stuff.

Not Colton and his diagnosis.

I mean, clearly he was high functioning, and his art was ridiculously good. But I also kind of felt like Googling information about the subject would be a little like *cheating* in this case.

There have been a lot of words to describe me over the years: precocious, hard-headed . . . indestructible. But I've never been known as nosy. There was a pamphlet lying in my hand explaining the smallest bits of information I could possibly have, and yet I couldn't bring myself to validate it. He'd been a regular little boy when we'd met. How was it possible that something was different about him?

I know better now. I'm not that naïve any more. But at the time, I didn't want to. I just felt drawn to him and like I wanted to know him better. Unlock his mystery on my own.

I think sometimes we're presented with the truth but we don't want to believe it. We see things the way we want to see them. Sometimes, we *choose* to live in denial.

* * *

After the fair, I waited until my parents fell asleep, which was probably eight o'clock because, let's face it, they're old, and then snuck out of the garage. The entire way to his house on my bike, I wondered what I was going to do. I just needed to see him. Don't ask me why. I just did. I remembered the way.

I crawled through the bushes around the side of his house until I was standing under the room I recalled was his.

It was the same room I'd taken the mattress from.

The lights were out and my heart kind of died right there inside my chest at the same time I had this horrible feeling of an over-full bladder that should have made me run away.

You know how hard it is to move when you have to pee that bad? Stupid nerves.

Instead, I moved around to the other side of the house and pressed my back against the far wall to see if the light was on in the room above the garage.

It was.

At fifteen years old, I was contemplating climbing the lattice that ran up the side of his house and swinging like a monkey over to the tree limb closest to his window. Just to get a glimpse of him. Just to be close enough to him to feel even a tenth of the kind of heart racing, blood-pumping excitement I'd felt in the less than ten minutes I'd been with him that day.

I wish now I would have done just that.

But I chickened out. Instead of being that badass girl I'd dreamt of being before I got hit by lightning, I turned around and went back home. To my room, where all my questions were still unanswered. Where my heart felt numb and empty all at once because I liked this boy and I knew nothing about his situation.

I just knew what it felt like when he'd said my name.

What it felt like to stand with him by the train tracks.

What it had felt like to have him walk away from me and leave me more confused than I'd ever been in my entire life.

That was the night I'd vowed to forget about Colton Neely because I was scared of what I might find out. My young brain came up with a million excuses as to why I was doing it, but I am honest enough with you now to say I was scared. It was within three months of that night that I met Joseph through his sister Tracy, and we started dating. Because he was interested and I thought he was cute.

He was my first real kiss and we had fun together, though nothing inside of me tingled or lit up like it had the day at the fair. In essence, I just went with the flow, ignoring any information about the artist I had known once upon a time, in another life. Here and there, I would hear he was opening an exhibit somewhere amazing. I would catch glimpses of his artwork as I turned the newspaper over to the comics to eat my cereal on Sundays.

Puddle Jumping

That void . . . that damn hole in my heart . . . it never really closed. Even after starting high school and becoming a member of the Debate Team so I could decide if being a lawyer was what I wanted to do. Even after helping Harper plan the school dances. Babysitting as much as I could to make extra money. Even after all that, there was still something missing.

I focused on trying to become a better person than the mean little girl who told a talented artist to color inside the lines all those years ago. It was kind of like floating in the middle of a swimming pool on a raft. Complacent. Happy because it was routine. It was life.

Harper and I hung out.

Joseph and I made out.

Homework assignments were handed in.

I was just there.

But life isn't really about just getting by. Right when you've lulled yourself into a false sense of security, it likes to throw in a plot twist. Keep you on your toes.

I had specifically not looked into Colton's 'condition'. And yes, I'm using finger quotes.

There was something inside me that didn't want to know. Something that made me think if I knew exactly what it was he was experiencing, then it would change my memories of him or sway me to look at him differently. And I didn't want that because the ones I did have of him, even when coupled with my near-death experiences, were pretty good. I felt *good* when I thought of him.

To have the knowledge of what was 'wrong' could have caused me to second-guess and analyze every last move he'd ever made. My interactions with him. His mother's sanity.

I was really, really good at pretending and ignoring things.

Weren't you?

Anyway. I'd had this misconception it meant he was handicapped. Obviously there would be a stigma attached to him, right? What I didn't know at the time was there are so many people on the spectrum that we're familiar with.

Like, celebrities.

You can look it up.

Would you ever know it? Probably not. But if you did, would it make you look at them differently? Would you scour their body language and everything to see if you can say, "Oh, yeah. That totally makes sense."

This is why I didn't want to know. I thought maybe I'd never see Colton again, and therefore, didn't need to spoil any of my precious memories of him.

I was a moron who feared knowing the truth would make things different in a negative way instead of positive. That it would be more than I could handle. But something I forgot about myself is that I'm pretty stubborn and loyal. Tenacious to a fault, in fact.

Later on, I figured out very quickly I'd do anything for him.

Anything.

I know it to be fact, because as soon as I'd nearly forced myself to forget about him, Colton Neely stepped through the doors of my high school on the first day of my senior year.

With a locker just a foot away from mine.

And he was even more beautiful in real life than he'd been in the faded picture I'd kept of him in the back of my mind.

chapter *four*

He was standing a foot away and I swear I almost passed out. It was like he was some sort of hallucination, but I had done one of those weird age-progression things they do on the news and my creative lobe took over making him much taller and so much more attractive because that would be *exactly* how my teenage fantasy would have played out.

Except he was so real.

I just stared at him for a second; breathing out of my mouth noisily and waiting for my alarm clock to sound, but it never came.

"Colton?" It had to have sounded like a question because I could hear the end of his name kind of lilting upward as it left my mouth and I sure as hell wasn't trying out a British accent, so . . . yeah, it must have been a question.

His eyes flicked to me and he nodded once, turning back to a paper in his hand.

"Hello." His shoulders were stiff and his chin was almost tucked into his chest as he took a moment to think. And just as abruptly as he appeared, he turned and walked away, holding his backpack strap tightly with one hand as he squeezed his other fist around the piece of paper.

Now, I had that little almost-stalking incident the last time I saw him, so I couldn't exactly fight my genetic makeup. So I tailed his ass, walking a couple people behind him until he veered off into a room I'd never really paid attention to before. There were already quite a few students inside, sitting at desks and chatting among themselves.

Well, except for Colton, who seemed to stall for a moment before finding an empty desk in the back corner.

Before I could gather my nerve to wave at him from the door to see if he would meet me in the hallway, I heard heavy footsteps behind me and turned just in time to see one of the senior football players rounding the corner, stopping before he almost slammed straight into me. He had hair that was almost white blond and big eyes that were crinkled with laughter at my slack jaw.

"Excuse me." He smiled and blushed a little, slipping by to walk into the room and be greeted by a couple friends.

I was so confused. Why would Sawyer Grant, football god, be in the same class as Colton? It didn't click with me that Sawyer could be like him, too.

Of course, now I know that's not the case.

Now I know he's dyslexic and has a hard time learning in regular classes.

I know the skinny brown haired girl who zipped by me to take her seat next to him is Marissa, and she has ADHD.

But that day I didn't know any of it until the bell rang and their teacher walked over to the door and shut it, proudly displaying the room name: Resources.

To say I was shocked would have been like saying boys like to touch boobs.

An *understatement*.

All of them looked fine.

I just remember wondering why Colton's mother had sent him to school just so he could be in a special class. She homeschooled him, didn't she? Which shows exactly how little I knew about anything, given the fact I was very self-absorbed and was always concentrating on *doing* good things to *look* like a nice person. But I was still judgmental and critical on the inside if I was having those thoughts.

Because not every kid who's in those classes is a stereotype.

Some kids just go once or twice a day.

Some kids go all day.

Some, I would learn, go by choice.

It really is amazing how much my thought process has changed since the beginning of my senior year of high school.

I remember just being in a weird daze as I made my way to my first class where Harper was already ignoring our teacher and reading a Cosmo because she claimed it pertained to her more than a Seventeen Magazine did.

What can I say? My bestie is a little . . . *advanced*.

"You're late," she'd whispered and I shrugged, settling into my seat and hoping not to be noticed.

"Colton Neely is here."

She laughed. "Yeah, I heard he enrolled. He was being tutored so he could do his art and stuff. I have no idea why he's here if that's true."

Word spread fast.

"God. How do you hear *this* stuff?"

Puddle Jumping

She shrugged. "I have connections in the front office."

It suddenly made all the sense in the world. And it was all I could think about through the rest of my morning classes, barely acknowledging Joseph when he grabbed my hand and pulled me toward the cafeteria. I hadn't needed to go back to my locker yet, and I was nervous as hell.

Colton had scarcely looked like he knew me.

While we were sitting at lunch and I was fighting this horrible nervous stomach cramp, I heard some whispers from across the table and looked up just in time to see Joseph's friends staring at a few people making their way toward a table along the far wall, away from the crowded middle section of the lunch room.

It was everyone I had seen in Colton's class, though I only recognized the few I saw walking by me that morning. There were so many of them occupying the lunch table, everyone taking seats like they were assigned.

Now, I'm pretty sure I was the only one at my table who knew Sawyer was in Resources with the other kids, which is why I was surprised to see him walking toward the table with his girlfriend, Quinn, like it was the most natural thing in the world. Marissa, I would later find out, was a grade below us, so I'd never had a reason to really pay attention to her before, and she sat down, too. Lastly there was Colton.

Joseph, with his dark hair and even darker eyes, tanned skin and recently braces free teeth, leaned into me. "Uh-oh. Look who just showed up."

You should have seen how red my face turned. I shrugged his arm off and turned to glare. "Don't be an asshole. You don't even know him."

He'd cocked this eyebrow at me. "And you do?"

It was like my lips were sealed with cement. "Just shut up, okay?" I'd said it as quietly as possible and instantly felt terrible. Nauseated at myself, I pushed away from the table and grabbed my bag. "I have to go to my locker before class."

Joseph offered to walk me but I said no because I needed a minute to just freaking *breathe*. He was pissing me off. And I was mad at myself for not saying yes to his question about Colton. So, I made my way down the corridors to my locker and pressed my head against the cool metal, wondering exactly what I was supposed to do.

"Lilly?"

It was that voice.

Oh, God. I love that voice.

23

"Colton."

I listened to him shift his feet from side to side for a second before I got the courage to look up. He stared at the floor for a beat and then he seemed to struggle with himself before pulling his hand out of his jeans pocket and offering it to me tentatively.

"Hello. I'm Colton Neely." His eyes flicked to mine and then to his extended hand.

I laughed a little. "I know." But he stood still I began to feel silly so I held out my hand and he flinched at the first contact, pulling back and scratching at his palm before thrusting it back into mine and squeezing. Hard.

"Why are you acting like you don't know me?" I asked, my heart now laying in a wet mess on the floor.

He released my hand and shoved his back in his pocket, his shoulders raising a little. "My dad said to be polite and introduce myself. He said I had to be polite."

It was then I realized just how hard this was going to be for him. He was so formal. So timid.

"You've always been polite," I whispered waiting for him to look up again. "Even when you were saving me from lightning."

His face shot up immediately at the memory and he blinked furiously. "You remember."

"Of course I remember. How could I forget? You saved my life." His eyes had widened further. "Twice," I reminded him.

He smiled then. Just a small smile, but it was all I needed before he let out a long breath and looked at the floor again. "You remembered."

The silence took over then, and I won't lie, it made me fidgety. So, I got my things from my locker and packed my backpack while he stood to the side, not saying a word. Finally, I had to break the tension.

"I haven't seen you in while."

His entire body language seemed to imply exactly how nervous he was. "Paint . . ." his mouth snapped closed and he looked down.

"Paint? Your paintings?" It was like pulling teeth.

His face grew solemn. "I'm only allowed to talk about painting three times today and I used my chances during first period."

Puddle Jumping

Something in my heart, now that it was back in my chest, stung as I looked at him because he seemed to be so embarrassed. He wanted so badly to do what he was used to.

I lifted my hand to touch him and then closed my fist by my side and looked up with my head tilted slightly. "I won't tell anyone if you don't."

My mind was chanting, 'Tell me, tell me, tell me.' Selfishly, I wanted to hear him speak. I wanted to hear his passion over something he loved.

It was, without a doubt, the best sentence to ever come out of my mouth in seventeen years.

He talked. Oh my God, did he talk. And I just stood there like a fool, smiling at him as he rattled off all this information so fast and excitedly, using words I'd never heard someone my age use before.

The bell rang and he was still going. I tried to cut him off, but there really was no stopping him once he'd started. I interjected long enough to get him to hand me his schedule in order to see about walking him to class. People may have walked by, staring at us, but I didn't pay any attention. I was in his world now, wrapped up in his passion, making my chest feel so damn full I thought I would stop breathing.

When he handed me his schedule, I felt tears rush to my eyes. You know that stinging in your nose right before the tears come? That's what happened as I realized we were headed to the same class.

AP English. Where our teacher had us all in alphabetical seating when we arrived. I watched Colton from my side of the room as he sat down and went stiff in the chest again, eyes forward and his mouth zipped shut.

About halfway through the period, Mr. Mercer began listing the names of the books we would be reading. I'd barely been paying attention at all because I couldn't stop staring at the back of Colton's head and the way his hair curled up at the nape of his neck . . . freckles trailing into his shirt.

I'd been so lost in my fantasy of actually touching them and wondering how it would feel to get my fingers wrapped around one wayward curl that I wasn't at full attention to hear Colton suddenly speak out to tell our teacher he had already read a few of them.

It was like an out of body experience watching his head raise a little higher as the words, low and steady just rushed from his lips.

Mr. Mercer had given him one of those *looks* and whispered that Colton needed to please raise his hand in the future before interrupting class with an outburst.

Poor Colton's fists curled in his lap and he kept his head down for the rest of the class, but as soon as the bell rang, I pushed my way to the front and tapped Mr. Mercer on the shoulder, giving him my very best authoritative voice as I told him flat out that Colton's mom had asked me sit with him during our class and he would move to the back row with me tomorrow. Mercer had given me a look like he didn't believe me, but I didn't back down.

An agreement was reached and I made sure to wait for Colton as we left class, knowing after seeing his schedule he was going back to the Resources room for another period.

He smiled a tiny bit when we reached the room, but turned abruptly and found his seat at the back of the class again. Like the creepy stalker-girl I am, I watched him settle in and then moved out of sight so he didn't know I was still there.

It was when I moved out of his view that I caught sight of the poster behind his head. It was of two pair of sneaker clad feet, one male and one female, frozen mid-air before landing in a deep puddle of water. Looking from their feet upward to their legs and higher, the shot revealed fingers knotted together as the boy and girl held hands. It was raining. It was black and white. And the only words on the poster were, *FRIENDSHIP: A true friend is one soul in two bodies – Aristotle.*

So cheesy, but all of that stuff in school is. Yet, this particular poster didn't seem that bad to me.

It made me wonder if it were true.

Puddle Jumping

chapter
five

After school, I completely ditched Harper and waited for Colton outside his last class. If he was surprised to see me, he didn't let on. Instead, he fell in by my side as if we'd been walking through the halls of our school together for years.

"Want a ride home?" I asked, my palms all sweaty again.

His head shook slowly from side to side. "At three-thirty-five I'm supposed to be standing outside for my mother."

I smiled as big as I could. "Then I'll wait with you."

A nod. That was all I got, but it didn't matter. It was something.

I'll be honest, I was more nervous about facing Sheila Neely again than I was to first approach her son. While we waited for her to drive the long loop set aside for car riders, mostly freshman, I thought of things I could talk to him about. Like, why the hell he was suddenly at school?

Instead, I chickened out. "Are you busy after school tomorrow?"

His answer was abrupt. "Yes."

Look, being a girl in high school is hard enough. But add having to do the 'dude' duty of asking someone to hang out was making my head want to implode. And we didn't want that.

About that time, his mom pulled slowly up before crawling to a stop. She rolled the passenger's side window down and then kind of pulled her sunglasses down the bridge of her nose as she squinted to see if I was really standing next to her son.

"Lilly Evans." The way she said my name made my nose scrunch. I said hello and she laughed, her head thrown back and reddish hair bouncing. "I didn't think you'd make it to *sixteen* . . . much less your senior year."

Touché, Mrs. Neely. One point for you.

Colton was getting into the passenger seat, blocking my view of her, so I moved around to her window. She'd smiled wide and pushed her glasses into her hair to address me. I was leaning in and trying to speak loud enough for both of them to hear.

"Would you mind if I picked Colton up for school in the morning? I can bring him home, too, if that's okay with you."

I swear on a stack of Bibles, her eyes got so wide I thought she was going to have a stroke.

"Really?"

"Yeah, really. He has a class with me and stuff, so I figured we could ride together and his locker is next to mine and then he wouldn't have to be dropped off and picked up."

She held a hand up to stop me and for a moment I thought she had tears in her eyes. "Absolutely."

"Awesome." It was like I could finally, *finally* breathe again. I was going to take care of Colton this time, not the other way around.

"He has a class tomorrow at the community college. Can you take him?" She looked so hopeful.

"Sure. Should I . . . sit in?" I couldn't remember if it was called shadowing or auditing or whatever, but neither of them sounded cool so I didn't push it.

Her voice . . . it got so low. "It's a socialization class to help him acclimate. You know, he wanted to do this on his own. He asked to come to school, but he doesn't *have* to be here." Her eyes actually did get shiny then. "He just wants friends."

"Don't worry, Mrs. Neely. He's already got one in me," I assured her and then leaned in a little to say goodbye to Colton. He nodded a couple times and they drove away, leaving me with a thousand questions.

It felt like everything that transpired on the day he started school was what I needed to prove to myself I should find out what I'd been putting off for *years*.

It finally felt like the right time to give in and find out everything I could about it.

I drove home immediately and Googled the shit out of Asperger's.

Holy hell. The amount of information available is so extensive. I couldn't tell which end was up. While he had some of the qualities and characteristics listed on the spectrum, he didn't seem to have all of them, and honestly, it just got to be pretty exhausting and confusing after a while. It made me want to lay my head down and cry because he was a complete mystery to me.

My research showed socialization was the hardest thing for someone like him to 'get'. Which made his after school class seem all the more necessary, obviously. But how could I help? At the time, I didn't think pushing him into school activities would be the right key.

What if he became over stimulated?

Would he freak out and have to leave?

Would he be absolutely fine and I was a total douche for thinking so many stupid questions?

Sometimes Googling things make it worse.

One thing was certain: I would do whatever it took to be what he needed me to be. He was worth it even after only one day.

* * *

About an hour before bed, I realized I had left my phone on silent and checked it to see about a million missed phone calls from Harper and Joseph. I was irritated to say the least. Harper would take a text, I knew. But Joseph was another matter altogether.

Calling him proved to be the second best thing I'd done that day. The conversation went a little like this:

"Hey. I missed your calls?"

"Yeah. What the hell were you doing with that Neely kid? Everyone saw it. They're all talking about you . . ."

I won't go into the specifics of what exactly was said, because it's . . . just . . . not important what people said about Colton or what they called him or categorized him as. But let's just say it was ignorant enough to warrant a kiss off of epic proportions.

In essence, I told Joseph he could kiss my ass.

We broke up. Over the phone. And it didn't bother me for a minute. Then my cell blew up with more texts from Harper.

I'll say it again: News travels fast.

But none of it mattered. Because I was finally seeing a little glimpse of who Colton was.

I slept well that night, knowing I'd be picking him up for school in the morning. Single.

The first time I picked Colton up for school, I got up early to put on a little more makeup. I straightened my hair a little extra. And I wore a skirt.

What can I say? My legs are *impressive*.

See, it wasn't that I had started out with the intention of having something more with him. It was like it was ingrained in me, somehow. He brought out this very basic desire in me to be a girl. A better girl. One who could hold the attentions of someone like him. So, it wasn't like I was thinking to go out of my way to do those things that morning, I just kind of did them because I wanted to.

Just because I was attracted to *him* didn't mean our friendship had to suffer. It was what would come first, regardless of my feelings.

I met Mrs. Neely at the door and I swear to you she took one look at my glossy lips and bare knees and the woman just *knew*. Moms are creepy like that sometimes. But I played it off and she pointed me to the room above the garage where Colton was rearranging some pieces.

It had been a while since I'd seen his stuff up close and it took my breath away at how far he'd come since the time I saw the paintings at the fair. Compliments tripped out of my mouth as I looked them over but he didn't seem like they really mattered. In fact, it wasn't until I mentioned a canvas that was broken in half and twisted in the corner of the room that he even really responded to me at all.

"What happened?" It just looked *mangled*.

Colton glanced at it and sighed, looking away again as he finished packing his book bag. "I was upset when I couldn't get the eyes right."

The brown edges of the picture were calling me to investigate further, but it was in my best interest to tone my stalking down, just a smidge, so I ignored it. Plus, he didn't seem like he wanted to talk about it. At all.

We rode together in silence that felt like a million pulses of static up my arms and neck. It was such a short ride that I didn't want to ask him more about art for fear I wouldn't get him to stop when we got to the parking lot, but according to my research, any other questions would have gotten me one word answers.

Like, "Do you like music?" could get a response of 'yes' and that would have been it.

It was such a stressful moment that I couldn't get my hands to stop shaking on the steering wheel and eventually talked myself into believing the silence was probably best so he could just get used to riding with me.

I'm not a very good driver, if I'm being completely candid.

The day went better than expected and by the time lunch rolled around I hadn't really given any thought to where I would sit. Harper had tried to talk to me in first period about

31

Joseph but I told her I didn't want to get into it at school. I wasn't really sure if she was going to try and strong-arm me into sitting at the table and force me to hash it all out in public.

Instead, she sent me a text right before I got there letting me know she was skipping out to meet with a junior in the parking lot.

I didn't even think twice about going to sit with Colton and his friends. I just did it.

Quinn's eyes darted back and forth between Colton and me a hell of a lot. She'd worn this knowing look on her face the entire lunch period as I pretended to listen to Marissa ramble and switch topics faster than a meth addict with a remote would change channels between hits. I smirked a little, too, when I noticed Colton's stare fixated on my thighs halfway through a conversation. It just reinforced the fact he was a regular boy, regardless of whatever obstacle he might have been born with that stopped him from showing it as boldly as someone else.

English was even better because I got to sit next to him as Mr. Mercer taught, and I could hear him talking under his breath every once in a while when the teacher said something wrong, or grammatically incorrect.

He'd clearly had some *incredible* tutors.

Butterflies exploded in my stomach when I drove him to his class at the college, and after walking him inside, it was determined it would be better for me to wait in the hallway so Colton didn't feel more awkward having me there. Everyone else in the room was on a level playing field. They could have jumped back a few steps in their progress with my presence.

I waited for the hour he was inside, playing on my phone, wondering what he was learning.

He appeared by my side immediately after the doors were opened, and he had this weird look on his face, like he was purposely unaffected. His hands were pushed into his pockets again and I remember vividly that the front of his yellow t-shirt was haphazardly tucked behind his belt buckle while he nodded toward me once in acknowledgement.

"Are you ready to go home?" I asked, wondering if I should take him straight there or offer to get him some dinner.

But his response made my mouth hang open in shock.

"Whatever."

I blinked and pressed my lips together, trying to form a response. "Whatever?"

"Yeah." He rolled his eyes. "Whatever."

Puddle Jumping

And then he looked at me and the corner of his mouth pulled up into a sly smile. "They taught us that tonight to help us blend in with our peers."

It made my heart leap out of my chest and I had to resist the urge to hug him and laugh all at once because he looked so damn cute and a little proud as he said it. Instead, I stood and gave him an awkward double thumbs' up of approval.

"You totally nailed it," I told him, my own smile creeping up on me until I couldn't hide it anymore.

It felt like the beginning of something incredible.

chapter *six*

I learned pretty quickly Colton's mind worked in literal terms and I would have to watch the way I spoke to him if I wanted to effectively communicate.

It was the small stuff that made me wonder how I could help him interact with other kids aside from his core group at the lunch table. *They* all seemed to know how to talk to him in terms he could work with. Well, except for Marissa who talked so fast I think Colton usually blocked her out like she was background noise or a humming in his brain. Especially since she never asked any questions.

It became my whole mission in life to make it as easy on him as possible. Maybe I should have thought about how hard it would be, but at the time I could barely even imagine it.

He seemed to settle into our new routine of me picking him up and dropping him off each day. Every time I would pull up to his house, I would chant in my brain for him to ask me to come inside. To invite me upstairs. But he never did.

A couple weeks later, after one of his PEERS classes, he sat on the ride home in his usual detached silence that I was becoming accustomed to.

I asked him how the class went and instead of answering he blurted out loudly, "Lilly. May I have your phone number to call you later this evening?"

Yeah, I was as shocked as you are. Believe me.

I said, "Of course." Followed by a very firm, "Yes."

It made me smile when he'd actually looked less tense after I answered. "Our homework is to start a conversation. I would feel most comfortable doing that with you, if you don't mind." Eyes still straight forward. Body language still stiff.

I said the only thing that popped into my mind. "You can do anything with me, Colton."

Trust me, he didn't quite get the innuendo, but my red as hell cheeks sure did. He just thanked me quietly and said goodbye as he exited the car, stating that he would call me at eight o'clock.

I was thrilled. Ecstatic, even. Girly squeals were trapped in my throat as I rushed into my bedroom and tried to focus on anything other than his impending phone call, but it was no use. I pretty much stared at my phone for two hours wondering if the AT&T satellite had actually bitten the dust, or if I had suddenly developed a dead space in my bedroom that was stopping me from receiving outside phone calls.

Turns out it wasn't either of those things. Colton simply needed to finish his nightly routine before attempting to call me. Any semblance of normalcy would kind of counteract going out of his comfort zone that night.

But he did call. He called at exactly eight o'clock. And after an initial awkward start, and feeling like I was going to pass out from lack of oxygen, we settled into a nice conversation. That night I realized he was just another seventeen-year-old boy, one who happened to be high functioning, and just wanted to be seen as a regular guy.

He trusted me implicitly to be his friend, and I was doing my best. But I was falling for him, and falling for him fast.

The realization made my heart hurt and also caused a sense of nervousness to settle deep in my gut. It came down to the simple truth that I could do all I could to learn about him and what he needed, but would it be possible for him to do the same?

Nothing in my life up until that point had even been close to being as confusing as that particular scenario. It was like it was happening inside me way too fast, yet it had been set up for seven years to be that way. He'd always been there, regardless of whether I allowed myself to think of him. I'd always been in the back of his mind, whether he could tell me that or not.

That evening we talked about music and I realized we basically had the same taste when it came to that, except he was also really into classical, which I waffled on learning about at some point. There were some things my brain just wouldn't accept.

He talked a little about movies, but it didn't seem to be something he was very interested in. He liked architecture, and of course, he loved art. I mentioned going to a museum and he'd barely responded so, I'd changed my approach by saying I would like him to take me to a museum one day. That seemed to do the trick and I made mental notes to converse with him in a no-nonsense and straight forward way. But I promised to never force him to do something he didn't want to do. I trusted that he'd say no if he needed to.

35

It would be hard for me, since I was used to being able to have people read the tone of my voice, or the look on my face. This was completely foreign to him. But it was a bit of a rush knowing I would be on the same uncharted ground as he was. We were almost on a level playing field at that point and it was scary but refreshing at the same time. I could learn right along with him. I could learn *him*.

I knew it didn't matter what other people said about me if I was going to pursue him in other ways. I just needed to know how to be strong in order to face any judgment that might occur. One thing was for certain, I needed to talk to someone who had been in the same position I was.

I didn't even have to ask. Quinn did first.

She walked by as I was leaving Colton in the Resources class and pulled on my arm. "Walk with me."

In the library, she sat me down across from her, tilted her head, and got straight to the point.

"You want to date Colton, don't you?"

"Yes." It was so nice not to hold it inside anymore. And then I started rattling off all of these questions about how I should go about it and the what-ifs involved. But right before I thought I'd run out of breath, she cut me off.

"Whoa. Hold on." Her hand was in the air again as I stopped mid-sentence and pressed my lips together. I clearly remember they were shaking and I worried I was going to bite straight through them if she didn't let me finish.

"You like Colton."

I nodded.

"And you want to date him."

I shrugged that time because it was too soon to say yes, but . . . hell yeah, I did.

"But you're afraid that . . . what? People are going to make fun of you, so you want my opinion on how to deal?"

It sounded so shallow, really. But I wanted Colton to be seen as more than this diagnosis, only I didn't know how to do it.

Her face was super serious while she thought. "Dating Sawyer isn't like dating Colton."

"I know. But no two couples are the same, right?" The knot in my stomach was making me nauseous because I didn't want to come across as a bitch about any of it. "Do any of your friends know Sawyer is in that class? Because I didn't have a clue before I saw him on the first day of school. And if so, how do they treat him? Or you? How do you make *them* see he's not different?"

It was then that she finally got it.

"The squad knows. His teammates know. And I think at first they were making fun of him a little, but he's not any different than he was before they found out. He's funny and smart." Her eyes on me made me pay closer attention. "You have no idea how smart he is. And kind."

"Is that why you eat at their table? Because I never noticed that before, either."

She nodded. "Sure. Why would you have? Not a lot of people go out of their way for them. But Sawyer will. He's all about breaking the stigma. We could eat anywhere in the cafeteria, but they're his friends. He's like a big brother in some ways and feels like it's his duty to set an example."

"That's exactly what I want to do." It was the truth. I wanted everyone to see how amazing they were. I already knew it. I was just waiting for everyone else to get a clue.

And then she said the most profound words I'd ever heard.

"You'd like to think it's a choice to love him, but it's not, Lilly. You've already decided. I can see it on your face."

I knew she was right. There was nothing inside me that could imagine it being any different. I wanted to be there with them and I didn't care what anyone had to say or who thought what about any of it.

"You want people to stop thinking he's different? Get him involved with your friends so they can see him like you do. Let them see the Colton you're falling so hard for. I guarantee they'll all get it in due time. He's really amazing." She smiled with that last sentence before leaving me alone in the library to mull over her words.

It was that night that I invited Harper over to discuss everything openly. At first, she seemed confused, thinking I had started to hang out with Colton out of some type of obligation because we knew each other when we were younger. And because he saved my life, twice.

"You broke up with your boyfriend in order to date Colton?" It was like I had given her a Rubik's cube to work on, she was so confused.

"I didn't say 'date' yet, but I'm really . . . I like him. A lot."

She nodded a little and then leaned back on her elbows to appraise me. "He's cuter than Joseph. But he's *weird*, Lilly."

"He's not weird. He's just not exactly like you. But, let's face it, neither am I. I think if I can get him to be comfortable around you and some other people, it would really, really help him come out of his shell and you'd see how incredible he is just like I do."

Right about the time I finished that sentence; she looked like she understood my intent. And it reminded me why we were friends in the first place.

"Then bring him to the bake sale prep tomorrow after school. Maybe he'll like helping us make cupcakes and cookies? It'll be social, I promise."

My heart swelled at her ability to just accept what I wanted and to be on board with me. I threw my arms around her, tackling her on top of my bed, thanking her over and over as I made plans in my head to proposition Colton to hang out with us the next day.

chapter
seven

It was a fine line to walk.

I mean, I could have *asked* him with the result being he immediately said no and went home to do his routine as he did every other night.

Or, I could *tell* him to come, but risk feeling like I was forcing him.

I was an utter wreck by the time I pulled up to his house the next morning. It wasn't something I wanted to ask him over the phone. Not that it mattered all that much if he could see my face when I asked. It mattered that I could see his.

Mrs. Neely ushered me through the front door and I greeted her as I did every morning. But instead of heading straight up the stairs to the art room, I decided to run it by her that I was planning on inviting Colton to stay afterward for the bake sale meeting. She seemed initially shocked, and almost a little worried.

"He may not like it, Lilly. Be prepared to have to leave. Quickly."

I was pretty sure I understood what she meant. "I know. I just want him to be able to do things other than his PEERS class and his art after school. You said he wanted to make friends . . ."

Her expression got really soft and she leaned in just a little closer than normal. I remember how gentle her fingertips felt against my cheek before she tucked a piece of hair behind my ear and then slid her palm under my chin to look into my eyes.

"Thank you," she'd murmured. "But, Lilly? Remember this is all new to him. And he's younger than you."

I couldn't hide the stupid blush in my cheeks as I'd replied, "This is new for me, too. And trust me, Colton's only younger than me in age."

She laughed and seemed satisfied I wasn't going into anything blindly. When I went up to his art room, I pushed the nerves aside and clenched my sweaty fists to gather my courage.

He was at the desk, packing his books. I knocked lightly on the open door and he gave me a small smile before zipping his bag closed.

It sounded so damn loud over the heartbeat in my ears.

"Colton?" My voice was shaking and I hated it but I pressed on. "Harper has asked me to bring you with me to work on some items for the bake sale after school today. Your mom said it was okay." He was just staring at me. "Will you come with me?"

He nodded. He decided he wanted to. It was enough for me.

School crawled by at half speed and I thought I would die if the last bell didn't ring because I was so worked up over how things could potentially go. I had made up a million scenarios in my head: good and bad.

But I knew Harper and there was nothing inside me that thought she would be anything but nice to Colton. He seemed more tense than usual when I met him at my locker, and as we moved toward the Home Ec room, I had to fight the urge to grab his hand and link our fingers.

I didn't know if he even liked holding hands.

It was so frustrating not knowing what he was thinking.

He was quiet as we walked into the room, and suddenly it felt like all eyes were on us. Scratch that. They totally were on us.

Harper raced over and pulled me in for a hug. And then she took a step back and looked at Colton, offering a genuine smile. "Glad you made it," she said.

"You're glad I made what?" Colton frowned and looked at her for explanation but she just shook her head and laughed.

"I'm glad you're going to be helping us ice these cupcakes," she corrected herself. And I was so effing proud of her for listening to the small tidbits of information I had given her the night before. She led us over to our table, where a few people were busy working on the sweets. Some were decorating and some were wrapping things in colorful plastic wrap. Others were boxing and writing on tags and I had to wonder what Colton would be most comfortable doing.

"Do you want to help put icing on the cupcakes?" I asked him as quietly as I could.

He said no because it was too sticky.

"What about gloves?"

Puddle Jumping

"Plastic and latex make my hands sweat and it's uncomfortable." His usual calm demeanor was starting to crack.

I leaned over and picked up a shaker of edible glitter for the tops of the colorful cupcakes. "Hold this," I whispered and watched as his fingers looped around the plastic container. "Is that okay?"

His eyes slid to mine briefly. "Yes."

"Good. Then, I'll ice the cupcakes and slide 'em to you so you can shake some glitter on top. But only a little bit. Like this." I showed him with my hand over his and my heart stopped beating when he started to pull back slightly. But he endured and I continued, knowing full well he would catch on fast. Which he did.

Within thirty minutes, we were lost in the redundancy of me icing and pushing the cupcakes over so he could sprinkle. Somewhere during that time, Harper came over to check on us. Then I noticed more of the girls were coming over to compliment Colton on his glitter shaking ability. Like he needed it. Frankly, it felt a little condescending.

He didn't really reply, given he was focused on the task at hand. But it didn't escape my notice the other girls seemed to be just a tiny bit too interested in him. Whispering a little too low at the other tables. When Harper came by again a few minutes later, I asked her what the hell was going on.

She leaned in close and told me all the girls were talking about how cute Colton was. How none of them had ever paid attention to him before, but his quiet nature and good looks were making the girls circle like sharks.

"'Cute' and 'hot' have come up at least twenty times." She chuckled, nudging my shoulder with her own.

And because I am me, I lost my footing and fell backward. Into Colton.

A shower of edible glitter rained down on my head and I looked up to see him staring down at me, his hands pushed up over his ears, as if he had no idea what to do. They were covered in pink sparkles, his palms leaving trails of it across his cheeks and up into his hair. It made me laugh because I knew I had to be a mess since the shaker had lost its top and bounced, showering me with the Herpes of Arts and Crafts.

It was such a damn disaster, and I started to laugh harder than I had in a very long time, struggling to stand and apologize to Colton. But by the time I made it up on my feet, I only saw the back of his head as he rushed out of the room.

41

Amber L. Johnson

I broke into a run, a trail of glitter falling from me with each footstep. "Colton!" I yelled down the hall for him, but he had his chin tucked and his button up shirt was open, flying behind him like some sort of super-hero cape.

When I finally made it to him, I jumped in front and held out my hands to stop him from walking away. He tried to move to the left, but seemed to be just as uncoordinated as I was, so he ran into me instead.

"You were laughing at me," he said, his neck veins bulging and jaw locked as his eyes avoided mine.

"No, I wasn't." I was trying my hardest not to raise my voice at him, but the lump in my throat made keeping my voice low almost impossible.

"You were."

I couldn't handle him thinking that of me, and in a moment of rash judgment, I did take his hand in mine, pulling us toward our lockers as he tried to back away. But my grasp only tightened further, and only once it reached an almost painful grip, did his hand stop trying to fight mine. It was like the harder I touched him, the less he tried to pull away.

Finally reaching my locker, I used my unoccupied hand to open it and pointed to the vanity mirror hanging inside. "You," I pointed to his reflection, "are covered in glitter." My hand pointed to my face and I finished. "Just like me. I did this. I fell onto you. Remember how I used to be?"

He blinked at his reflection and looked at me before nodding.

"It hasn't changed. I just don't get hit by lightning anymore." With every shake of my head more glitter spilled to the floor.

And suddenly he smiled, his gaze raking over the sparkly shit all over my head, face, arms and hands. It traveled the length of my torso until it landed on our sparkle covered palms. Clasped tightly together.

With a small sigh he squeezed my hand tighter. "I wish you were like me."

The breath in my body just rushed out all at once as I asked him why.

His gaze traveled my face again before he focused on my hair, saying exactly what he had on his mind. "Because then you would understand."

* * *

Puddle Jumping

It was those words that made me fall in love with him. Right there in that spot. Because he wanted me to be like him. That was *his* normalcy.

And I knew exactly what he meant.

When I drove him to his house, I didn't wait to be invited inside. I just went. His mom looked like she was about to shit a brick over the amount of glittery fairy dust we trailed in. But his dad, Rick, just laughed. I'm sure I had a guilty look on my face or red cheeks or something because they kept staring at me as I told them about what had happened while Colton was busy upstairs taking a shower, washing stuff off to the best of his ability.

Mr. Neely, dark hair and kind eyes, finally took advantage of a pulse of silence to clear his throat and asked me what I had been up to over the past seven years. It caught me off guard and I did that weird mouth thing I'd been doing around Quinn the day before, which only made Mrs. Neely laugh harder because her son, the one who was diagnosed with having a disorder of some kind could speak eloquent sentences and I couldn't even make my lips work.

The reason I was so flustered was because I knew there was something great starting between me and Colton and I wasn't sure how his parents felt about that. There's always the off chance they know that something more is progressing. And while I wasn't about to pull out a business card with my name and "Certified Virgin" printed on it, I almost wanted to just so they would feel comfortable with me being alone with him. Seriously. I was giddy and rattled from *holding his hand.*

I imagined kissing him would probably send me to the hospital. Again.

They ended up asking me to stay for dinner but I wasn't quite sure Colton would like me messing up his schedule even more that day. So I hedged a little, telling them I needed to check with my parents. And right when I was about to excuse myself to call my mom and get her stamp of approval before approaching Colton about it, he appeared at the bottom of the stairs.

"Colton? We've asked Lilly to stay for dinner," Mrs. Neely called to him.

It was like I did one of those cool-ass slow motion tricks from the movies. You know, the kind where I would turn and my hair would fan out all around me and land beautifully on my back as sparkle dust plumed outward and onto their fine cherry floor. I'd lock eyes with Colton and he'd smile and nod, extending his hand toward me like we were in some fairytale.

Well, it was kinda like that. But not really. Okay. Not at all. Instead, I turned too fast and tripped over my feet, sending my elbow into the banister next to the door. Hard.

Mr. Neely was on his feet immediately and rushed over to see if I was okay and I shrugged it off while trying not to look as embarrassed as I felt. I rubbed my elbow and tried not to cry.

Colton gave his mom an animated look and nodded his head. "Then I'll hide all the scissors and chewing gum." It made the entire room grow quiet before he looked over at me. "I know how upset you were last time when I had to cut your hair."

My jaw was on the floor. He'd totally cracked a joke.

"Then I guess you should hide the *mattresses*, too," I shot back playfully.

The silence that followed that statement made me want to crawl in a hole and die. Because Colton may not have gotten the innuendo . . . but his parents sure did.

That started my weekly dinners with the family. I didn't push him into inviting me, but waited on one of his parents to extend the invitation instead. He never objected and I really loved seeing him at his house because he was so much more relaxed. I saw a side of him there I didn't get to see at school when he was trying to focus on what he was expected to do.

The impressive thing about school was the more I hung out with him, the more people started to really see him, too. Especially the girls. Because, let's face it, a cute boy is a cute boy, whether he's all that different or not. This made it easier for him in his other classes, since people were warming up to him. But it made it all that much harder on me because I was constantly wondering if he enjoyed their company and conversation more than mine.

Though, once he started holding my hand, he never really stopped. Our palms were like ultra-strength magnets that just slapped together every time we were in each other's vicinity. We held hands. Hard. Always. Up and down the halls of the school. After school. In the car. Hands and fingers.

Always touching.

Puddle Jumping

chapter eight

The start of any relationship is really la la la and happy-happy, right? I mean, I'm a teenager for God's sake. And so is he. So, there are hormones involved and all kinds of crazy things adults never really tell us about . . . at least not in words we can understand.

I can go from ecstatically happy to massively insecure in the span of a second. I can go from feeling completely at ease with Colton, to wondering if I'll do anything right ever again.

It's hard to be level headed when I can barely control my thoughts, much less my impulses.

Teenage girls are stupid.

I can say that because I am one. And I know we're all competitive with one another, even if we pretend not to be. We totally are.

Every damn day I walked into school I was aware that the blondes with the perky boobs and the bubble butts get the guys. I was aware my best friend is one of them. And I was painfully aware that I am skinny, but jiggly, and the definition of average-brown-hair-brown-eyed girl.

But when Colton talks to me or looks at me, I feel really special. Prettier than I've ever felt before in my life. I figured the other bitches in school would see that, too. I assumed they would know, since we held hands all the time, and drove to and from school, walked to class and ate lunch together: Colton and I were, ya know . . . *together*.

Apparently, I was wrong.

The simple fact that neither Colton nor I had actually said we were boyfriend and girlfriend made people think maybe we weren't. We hadn't kissed or anything, and I guess a lot of people . . . girls . . . saw me as just some sort of friend or something. Friends who hold hands?

As Colton would say, "Whatever."

He'd gotten better at chiming in with little things here or there that would catch us all off-guard at the table. Unprompted.

Puddle Jumping

Girls were suddenly trying to talk to us during lunch, but couldn't quite get a grasp on Colton's reactions or silence. It made Quinn laugh to no end, and Sawyer sat back with a shit-eating grin on his face because he could tell I was like a tiger about to pounce every time one of them came over. Marissa would usually interject and talk the girls' ears off and they'd eventually make an excuse to walk away.

Anyway. We got the announcement about the Girls' Choice Dance and all the girls in the school suddenly got lobotomized or something because half of them were crying about having to ask a boy out and the other half were making lists. Those that didn't have boyfriends, that is.

I hadn't really been paying attention to what was going on, oblivious to gossip sessions around me for a couple weeks, thinking it was obvious to everyone I would be asking Colton to the dance, when I heard the first rumor.

No less than three girls had vocalized their intent to ask him.

Now, you have to remember I was the only girl to have spent copious amounts of time with him alone. With his family. Learning how he ticked. So, I definitely had the advantage there. It was almost like I wanted to see these other girls crash and burn when they asked him to take them to the dance.

But another part of me didn't even want them to get the satisfaction of asking.

I had a mini panic attack because I wasn't sure if the dance would be too loud. Too crowded. Too much stimulation.

Would it even be worth trying to go?

One look at him as he came out of class that day answered every question I had in my head. *Of course it was worth it.*

Like that crazy bitch from *Kill Bill*, it was like I could see girls were approaching from everywhere, and it appeared they were all coming at us at once in some sort of race against time to get to him first. Right in front of my effing face.

"Colton?" I grabbed onto his hand tightly and turned his back toward the locker, getting his attention focused only on my face. "I want to ask you a question." He nodded. "Take me to the dance next weekend."

He tilted his head to the side and frowned. "Lilly, that was not in the form of a question. A question is a request that ends with a question mark. What you just said was a statement."

47

Amber L. Johnson

"Will you take me to the dance next weekend?" My heart was about to jump out of my throat wielding a sharp knife to cut the Achilles tendons on the approaching bitches' feet.

But Colton was just staring at me.

"I'd like you to take me to the dance. Please?"

He chewed his lip. Blinked a few times. Appeared thoughtful.

And right at the moment the first girl made it to us, he gave a shrug. "Okay."

Triumphantly, I whirled around and mouthed, 'Too late'.

I was stupidly giddy for the rest of the day. I was victorious.

And then I remembered I hate to dance.

No matter. I would go with Colton and we would be together in public and it was really all that mattered.

Harper let me borrow a dress and I let her do my hair and makeup before driving over to meet him so our parents could take our pictures. Parents are so weird about that kind of stuff anyway, and my dad was giving him the sly eye while the moms ran around taking pictures and talking about how cute we were. And all the while, Colton . . . more handsome than ever before in a suit . . . a black suit and white shirt . . . hair meticulously combed, blue eyes wide . . . never stopped looking at me.

He didn't need to say he thought I looked nice. I saw it in his face.

The red dress I wore made me feel pretty. Colton's stare made me feel downright beautiful.

By the time we walked through the doors of the gymnasium, music blasting and lights popping from camera flashes and little disco balls hanging from the ceiling, I thought my hand would fall off. Colton was squeezing it so tightly; I swear my fingertips were turning black.

Yet, he endured. I made sure to walk him through the crowd of sweaty dancers and by the tables of kids who thought they were too cool to be there. We waved at our friends but continued walking because Colton was seriously experiencing too much stimulation, so I did what I figured would be best.

I pulled him outside to the white tent behind the building. It was lit with pretty white lights and the girls who decorated had hung Japanese lanterns across the ceiling. It was cute. It was cheesy. It was romantic in a funny way, and I couldn't help but smile as I led him out there where the music was lower, the lights were softer, and only one other couple was hanging out, drinking soda.

I turned and looked up into his face, moving my arms up to his shoulders and started swaying a little. Just side to side. I'm a terrible dancer, but these things are special and I wanted the memories with him.

He was stiff, as usual, but I didn't mind. His hands didn't really know where to go, so I placed them on my hips and rested my cheek against his chest, just closing my eyes and inhaling how amazing he smelled with his shirt starched and some kind of deodorant that smelled like lickable-boy.

He seemed *too* quiet and I wasn't really sure what to do about it. I was just as nervous as he was, you know?

I lifted my head to see him staring down at me and I could only offer a shy smile and a laugh. "Colton?"

"Yes?"

I tightened my linked fingers around his neck. "Tell me about Monet."

So he did and it was music to my ears. To my heart. He talked so passionately about the things he loved and I ended up resting my head against his chest to hear him speak through his sternum, all low and rumbling.

Bass and baritone laced between heartbeats and short breaths.

Suddenly . . . he stopped.

My head shot up and I looked at him, curious as to why he went silent. Of course I asked because that was how it had to be.

"Why'd you stop?" My throat was all dry because of the intensity between us. Like the air had suddenly gone thin and was replaced with pure energy.

He looked at me and then away a bunch of times and somehow I just knew what was about to happen, but my brain and hormones were off kilter and I just stood there like a moron waiting for him to speak.

Instead, he closed his eyes and leaned forward, his forehead kind of pushing mine back as he breathed quietly outward onto my face. I closed my eyes and just let it happen.

He kissed me.

Warm and soft. Gentle at first until his lips had acclimated to mine. It wasn't like any kiss I'd ever experienced before because my knees felt nonexistent and I wanted to fall, taking him with me in a pile on the ground so I could curl into him and never let go.

49

He was shaking and then grew more confident as I parted my lips and caught his in between mine.

We both pulled away at the same time. I must have been bright red and he, I know, he was flushed, all hard breathing and starting to sweat a little from the tension. But I didn't care. He'd totally kissed me. And it was amazing.

I didn't even mention the fact he was pretty much feeling up my left boob with his thumb. I just moved a little and maneuvered it away so I didn't draw attention.

"We should do that again," he mumbled and looked away into the white lights above my head.

I just held him tighter while I whispered, "Any time."

* * *

I've said it before but it bears repeating: Colton is very literal. I told him he could kiss me anytime. He did just that. It was cool on the one hand because he wasn't one of those guys who was an asshole and had to look out for his appearance in front of others. It was a drawback on the other because sometimes he did it without warning, like in the middle of a conversation.

I often wonder if there's judgment directed at me because of the physical relationship I have with him. If there's a stigma attached to me that I'm taking advantage of him.

I'm not, if you're wondering.

Like I said, no matter what a doctor once said about him, he's still a teenage boy. And that's pretty standard across the board, if you catch my drift.

What I'd like to really stress about this is when you love someone, their differences fall away. I don't look at him and see anything but *him*, and how sweet he is. I know how my stomach erupts in excitement when he simply holds my hand. How my heart reacts when we kiss. I know, above anything else, that when we're together, it's because we both want it. Not because of any other reason.

The one thing I wish I could explain to people is he's not what they think he is. Words he's been branded with could never describe him. He's not special. He's extraordinary. To me.

And I feel like I am, too, when I'm with him.

* * *

I was glad we had gone to the dance together because it was basically a back to school thing, being only six weeks into the year. The next dance was Homecoming, and I'd learned Colton was going to be attending the opening of one of his shows that night, so he wouldn't be able to make it at all. Mrs. Neely invited me to join them and the decision was easy to make.

One night after I ate dinner with his family, we went up to the art room and I took a look around at some of his newer pieces while he cleaned up from dinner and changed into some clothes that could be ruined if paint flew. I really loved the way he looked in his painting clothes. He was at ease. Comfortable.

The art room above the garage was his safe place and I still couldn't believe he trusted me so much to let me in.

That he was going to trust me to watch him work.

I wandered through the room looking at the canvases when I remembered he had that one painting in the corner that had been trashed. It wasn't there anymore so I continued to walk the outer walls and move the art around so I could see them more clearly. My attention was on some of the more abstract ones and I was flipping through them carefully when I stopped cold.

I was staring right into a perfect replica of my face.

"Holy shit on a stick." I probably said it louder than intended because I heard Colton's feet pause in the hall before they came to rest behind me a foot away.

"I couldn't get the eyes right," he'd said quietly and I turned around to look at his face, completely and utter flattered and breathless at what I held in my hands. "The other one. I couldn't get the eyes right. That's why I broke it."

"It's perfect," I whispered and turned to look back over at the picture. "You made me look really pretty." The words were hard to say but they were true. He'd captured something with his brush I'd never seen in myself through the reflection of a mirror.

"I believe I got the symmetry correct this time." His feet shuffled a little on the carpet.

After a moment, I turned back to him and offered a smile, unsure why there were tears in my eyes. But he noticed them and looked a little caught off guard.

"Did it upset you?"

"No." I wiped the ridiculous tears away and shook my head.

"Is there something I should do?" It was that question that made my heart crack down the middle and I started crying for real, just overwhelmed with all the feelings I was experiencing and not quite sure of them myself. "Lilly?"

51

Amber L. Johnson

I had finally gotten up the nerve to ask the question I wanted the answer to "Am I your girlfriend?"

"Of course." Like it was the most obvious thing in the world.

His answer made my heart soar and I just sort of stepped forward and blinked up at him . . . and asked him to kiss me.

chapter
nine

That little shy smile of his pulled up one of his cheeks and he met me halfway, dipping his face to plant a kiss on my lips. Once. Twice. And the third time, I got brave and pulled on the back of his neck and opened my mouth to . . . ya know . . . slip him a little tongue.

I was in the moment and wasn't thinking clearly, so it hadn't occurred to me he might think it was gross or whatnot, but he'd pulled back a little and frowned, making me feel weird and self-conscious.

"I'm sorry. Was that gross?" I asked, wanting to melt into the floor and just die.

He shook his head slowly and then looked at me for a second. "I'd like to try this after you've brushed your teeth."

Oh my God. So embarrassing.

Now, if he were any other guy, I would have probably hit him. Somewhere. Face. Arm. Nuts. But he was *Colton* and he was brutally honest about everything and had no filter to stop it, so my only reaction was to laugh and step back, assuring him I would brush my teeth next time.

Then he caught me off-guard again. "My mother keeps extra toothbrushes in the guest bathroom for my grandparents when they visit."

I couldn't get down the hall fast enough. His parents were still downstairs and they'd never had a reason to come up to the room before, so I wasn't worried about Mrs. Neely catching me freshening up. What I didn't account for was Colton coming to watch me from the doorway.

"Are you checking to see if I brushed correctly?" I joked and then realized he actually was when he intently watched me rinse. I felt like maybe I needed one of those little white mirrors on a stick the dentist uses so he could count my fillings.

I smiled and pointed at my teeth. "All clean. Will you kiss me now?" He just stared at my mouth and I felt dumb asking, but it was getting claustrophobic being in that little space. He took a step into the bathroom, making me take a step back to settle against the sink. I'd invited him in, so I'm not sure why it shocked me as much as it did. I guess it was just the way he was coming at me.

I was used to him holding his hands by his sides or gripping onto the belt loops of my jeans. But this time he held my cheeks in his palms, firm and rough while he moved in to kiss me again. I had no qualms about slipping my hands up into his hair to fist it because I knew he liked being touched a little harder than most.

My tongue flicked out again and his snuck out a little to touch it and somehow, somewhere in the universe, a switch got flipped on because he was really into it within seconds. My whole body reacted and I angled into him to hold on for dear life as he attacked me with his mouth, over and over again in unrelenting sweet torture.

Then it happened.

His hands weren't on my face anymore. They were on my chest and he was groping me so roughly I had to pull back and I'm pretty sure I said, "ow," because he was immediately off me with his back against the wall looking as if he had done something wrong.

"Did I hurt you?"

I shook my head and then nodded once. "It was a little too hard." My mouth almost felt bruised and I faintly tasted blood. "But it's okay." I wanted to assure him so he wouldn't be scared to try it again. "Come here," I motioned for him and he stepped forward so I could shut the door behind him.

"Are you aroused? I am."

I did actually laugh at that because he was so blunt sometimes I had no other choice but to do so.

"Yes." I pulled him closer and took his right hand in my left, squeezing it to let him feel safer. "Very." I was a ball of excited girl and he was my boyfriend and, yes, we were in the bathroom at his house . . . but it didn't matter.

I stepped up on my tiptoes and kissed him firmly again, his hand still in mine. His eyes closed and he stiffly kissed me back.

"Relax, Colton," I whispered between kisses. It took a moment before he did and once he had loosened up and gotten into the rhythm of kissing again, I parted my lips inviting him in for the next step.

We concentrated there for a good minute until I could feel him getting warmed up again and hesitantly, I pressed his open palm to my chest.

Puddle Jumping

I knew him. I wanted him.

It felt really, *really* good.

It was too much for me so it had to have been too much for him. I took a deep breath and leaned away, giving him one last kiss before slipping his hand back down to my waist.

"Are you all right?" I asked and he opened his eyes, droopy lids and hot breath accentuated by pink cheeks.

"Yes."

A smile. A nod. Another small kiss.

"I should go." I had planned on staying to watch him paint, but the tension was too thick and I didn't think I'd last an hour more in his room, watching him work.

He stood in the doorway for a second and said goodbye before shutting the door on me. I made sure I looked presentable before escaping his house like my ass was on fire.

* * *

It never occurred to me that people thought a certain way about Colton. Like, if they didn't know him and he did something they would consider to be strange or rude, you could see their faces turn bitter and I could almost hear them thinking he was a jerk for not initiating conversation or looking at them when speaking. Or, if he became easily distracted by something that caught his interest, others would seem to think he was ignoring them.

But as soon as it was brought to their attention that his brain worked differently, they just accepted it and after that it was, "Oh, Colton is a wonderful young man. He's just a little different. He doesn't make eye contact and he hugs too hard."

Colton doesn't care about things like that. He cares about art and making friends. He works in a space within his mind that allows him to do what he wants to, without feeling like he's wrong for it. There are no rules as far as his passion is concerned. And I envy him.

I wanted, more than anything, to take his paints and stand in his art room in just my underwear and throw buckets of colors at a canvas just to see what kind of chaos would bleed down the face and mix to make new shades of colors that possibly hadn't even been invented yet.

But I didn't.

Because I don't have it in me.

I ate dinner weekly at his house and spent time with his family. I always took him to and from his PEERS classes. I never really minded that he didn't call me every night, and that we didn't go out on real dates. What Colton lacked, I tried to

55

overcompensate for. He would most likely never be interested in the things I liked, but if I could meet him on his same ground, then we'd have a chance. I was sure of it.

I drew the line at learning about architecture because that is just boring. You can't say I didn't try, though.

We could hang out for a short time after school with people in small groups that he was comfortable with. But he seemed to really be most at ease when it was just the two of us, and I can't say it bothered me at all to have alone time with him.

What I had failed to realize during all of that was, even though I was going out of my way to see things through his eyes . . . to understand him more and more each day in order to make our relationship work . . . learning about things was not enough.

There's a huge difference in reading about it and experiencing it.

* * *

The night of the Homecoming dance, Colton had an art exhibit downtown. I got all prettied up in a new dress my mom gave me money for. I bought new shoes, did my hair, and even wore a little more makeup than usual. I did all of that because I was going to be seen with Colton in public at one of his shows and I wanted to present myself the best way I knew how.

He looked incredible, as always, in a casual suit and I couldn't take my eyes off him the entire ride downtown. Nor could I hide the immense pride and happiness I felt when he took the stage, looking bashful and blushing, to acknowledge the crowd with a couple short sentences, his eyes focused on the exit sign at the far end of the room.

People clapped and fawned all over his work and I hadn't really thought about the fact he'd taken the portrait of me and hung it as well. The people who passed by would look the picture over and then their attention would fall on me and I would get these strange looks. It made me very uneasy to think people were being judgmental about our relationship by thinking I was with him for any other reason than being in love with him. Like I was, as my mom would say, hitching my wagon to his star.

It made me uncomfortable and, after a while, I moved to the back of the room and waited at a table, people-watching.

But that feeling of insecurity was nothing compared to the pit I got in my stomach when my gaze had roamed the room for Colton and found him in the farthest corner next to the stage . . . speaking one-on-one with a gorgeous girl who reminded me of a young Nicole Kidman. She was tall and slender with light, almost red, curly tresses.

Jealousy flew through me faster than I'd ever thought possible. I was on my feet, crossing the room with my stare deadlocked on him. But when I arrived by his side, he didn't seem to acknowledge I was there. Neither did the girl.

It wasn't until Mrs. Neely swept by us that she stopped their conversation and introduced me to Talia Benton, a girl Colton had been chatting with online in an Asperger's forum, as he had been instructed to do by his PEERS teacher.

My heart once again felt frail and useless in my chest because I fully understood at that moment that all my good intentions were for nothing if I was just trying to learn about Colton's likes and dislikes. The reality of it was it was not the same as being like Talia.

She got it. She probably understood the way Colton thought. She totally got how he felt.

Because she was the same.

And for the first time, I wished I was too.

chapter ten

The ride home was torturous.

In most relationships, you can say to the person: *Who was that? How long have you been talking to her? Do you want to be with her?*

That just wasn't the case with us, and it was killing me not to be able to address what was making me feel so horrible inside.

He held my hand. He talked art and answered his parents' questions with an unusual amount of excitement. I was trying my hardest not to cry, but it was out of character for him to be so vocal and my only thought was Talia's presence had made him that way.

When we arrived back at their house, he got straight out of the car and headed inside. Even though my heart was breaking, I started to follow him. But Mrs. Neely stopped me before I made it to the door, asking if we could chat.

Now, my first thought was Colton had somehow slipped that he'd been all over my bunny slopes and she would be mad and tell me we needed to only visit with supervision. My head was spinning all over the place with misplaced anxiety and the fresh pictures in my head of Talia, so tears were welling in my eyes as she led me to the side of the house where the porch swing was and took my hand to sit me down.

What I didn't expect was for her pat my hand softly and sigh before she wiped one of my tears away.

"Are you okay?"

She asked it like she really cared and I could only nod because I was afraid using my voice would cause me to start wailing like a psycho. Apparently she didn't believe me. I wouldn't have, either. I'm a terrible actress.

"I should have told you that she was coming. I don't know why I didn't think about it affecting you." Her eyes were soft, like she meant it. "You're so good with him. *To* him. He's grown exponentially over the past few months just by having you around. You should know that."

"I don't know if it's enough."

58

Puddle Jumping

She nodded, all-knowing and Gandhi-like.

"Then let me say it for him, since he can't." She smiled a little. "Yet." Thoughtfully, she held my hand tighter, reminding me of her son. "He talks about you all the time."

Panic hit me pretty hard and I braced myself for the discomfort I was sure to experience when she started talking about my boobs.

"He talks about you to *us* because he's not going to talk about you to *you*. He talks to *her* online because his teacher suggested it. But that girl is obsessed with Math and Physics. It bores him no end, but he does it because he was told to in order to reach his end goal. The reason she was there tonight was because it was part of his homework to invite her into a social setting."

"But she's *so* pretty," I finally managed to get out before my voice cracked.

Mrs. Neely's eyes were shining and she smiled again. "Sure, she's pretty. But Colton didn't say one thing about that when she left. He said she was . . . what was it?" She thought for a moment and then giggled. "He said she was unnaturally tall for a girl her age. And that she smelled like chlorine."

It made me laugh, too, because I could hear him saying it in my head.

She took my chin in her hand and pulled my face up to look at hers. "He *painted* you. It's as close as he'll get to saying how much he cares for you right now. I knew the day you came to play with him all those years ago that you would be good friends, Lilly. It just wasn't the right time. Everything he lacks, you have. Spirit. A sense of adventure."

My tears had almost dried before they started up again and I'd nodded thankfully, trying to look away from her but she wouldn't let me.

"You're the reason he wanted to go to school. He's never forgotten you. And he thought he'd see you again if he went."

It didn't make sense, really. Coming to school was putting him in the position to be made fun of and be anxious. Why would he do all of that?

"So many times, more than I can count, he'd ask. 'Where's Lilly?' And I'd have to tell him that you were probably at school. Eventually he just asked what school you were in and if he could go, too. Please don't get upset, but I made sure you were there before I agreed. How could I say no? He's been in occupational therapy. I paid a lot of money when he was younger to get him into a room with other

59

children to make friends under the watch of a therapist. If you haven't noticed, he's much more comfortable with adults. But you? He wanted to find you again. He doesn't care about what others think about him. Spending time with those other people in his class has been an added bonus. But you're the reason he continues to go."

Call me blindsided, but I'd had no idea.

"I was so surprised to see you standing at the pick-up with him on the first day. I thought it would take more than a few hours for him to find you and become friends again. But you've always had a good heart, even if you're clumsier than anyone else in the world. Anywhere. Ever."

I wanted to laugh but I needed answers. "Is that why you said I couldn't hang out with him anymore when we were younger?"

Her eyes dropped to where our hands were still joined. "I was seriously afraid you were going to kill yourself on our property . . ."

At that point we both started laughing because it was the truth. Had I been left alone with him any longer, Colton would surely have been present at my funeral.

"It's been a really tough road for us. From the minute I knew something was different about him. Between the testing and evaluations, learning him and how he works . . . I've often thought maybe I did things wrong. That he should have been in school this entire time. But it's just not for him. He gets frustrated when he can't communicate because the other person isn't on his level. He touches too hard. He gets overwhelmed and it makes him break down because he can't vocalize what's happening inside of him. Having the tutors alleviated some of that.

"Maybe I should have told you when you were younger. But if I walked into every room announcing that he wasn't the same as everyone else, it wouldn't have done him any favors. I want people to see him for who he *is*. All I've ever wanted was for him to have some semblance of a normal childhood – a normal life. When you came around, I thought maybe, because he was so enamored with you, that you two would be a good fit. You've never judged him. I'm overprotective to a fault because of what we've been through, and it was a rash decision to remove you from his life, but I felt it was best at the time. But he never forgot you. Not for one day. There are paintings upstairs that prove just that. And if you can hold onto that truth for the future, when things get tough and you're feeling like it's a little one-sided, then maybe it won't be so bad."

This was the truth he could not say, and it made me happier than I ever thought I could be.

She released me and I made my way up to his room to tell him goodnight. And though I was torn to leave him, I knew I had to walk out the front door. But before I did, I snuck into the art room to unlock his window.

Because it would be the first night I would climb that lattice to sneak into his room after his parents went to bed.

* * *

I was nervous as I pulled my car around to the other side of his neighborhood and parked off the road before changing into a pair of sweatpants, t-shirt and flip flops I kept in the car for emergency sleepover clothes when I would hang out with Harper.

The night made every sound of my feet on dead leaves become magnified by a million percent. I had to bite my lip to stop from mouth breathing and causing white puffs of smoke to give me away as I snuck through the yard of his neighbor directly behind him.

And I'll have you know once I reached his house on foot, I made that lattice my bitch.

There's something about being focused and motivated that can give you an adrenaline rush unlike anything you've ever experienced before. That was what happened as I pulled myself up the unsteady and flimsy wood and pushed the window open to slide inside. At first I was worried I would fall and land on one of his pieces he was still working on, but I didn't and pride kind of surged through me, making the experience all that much better.

All the lights in the house were off save for the one in his room farther down the hallway. I let the minimal glow lead me to his door and stood off to the side so I could compose myself before knocking quietly. He didn't call out a response, but I heard his footsteps and when the door did open, he froze and stared down at me, bewildered.

"May I come in?" I whispered and he tilted his head to look me over.

"Did you forget something?"

I laughed nervously and took a deep breath. "I snuck in the window. I wanted to see you."

"You should have used the front door." He was still just staring at me.

Amber L. Johnson

How was I supposed to explain?

"I know I should have, but I didn't want your parents to know I was here. I wanted to see you."

"You already saw me today."

It was all I could take. "I wanted to kiss you some more, if that's okay."

He smiled. "You should have said that first."

I shuffled into his room as quietly as possible and stood off to the side of his bed while he leaned against his desk, clearly unsure of what we were supposed to do.

That made two of us.

Did I mention the fact that he was shirtless? In only pajama bottoms?

I think it was the first time I had seen him like that and I'm not ashamed to admit I was staring a little.

My boyfriend is gorgeous to me. And shirtless he's even more worthy of a lattice climb.

His computer screen caught my attention and I fought back the urge to ask him if he was talking to Talia. What his mother had said was true and I needed to believe that in order to keep hope that everything was going to be good between us.

"Colton?" I slipped off my flip-flops and dug my hand into my pocket. "Can I use your toothpaste?" My hand thrust forward with the toothbrush I had with me, and he grinned, nodding and pointing to his bathroom. He watched from the door as I did my routine before I moved into the bedroom and sat on his bed, suddenly feeling very shy.

He was by my side immediately, his mouth pressed to my neck and fingers pulling at my waist. But I angled away a little and held his hands in my lap as I got the words together I wanted to speak. "I need to ask you something."

"Yes?"

"I have to ask. Why do you like me?"

He shifted away from me then, his brows pulled together making him look even cuter, if that was possible. "I don't understand the question." His hands were squeezing mine tightly as he looked down at them. "You're my Lilly. You've always been my Lilly."

My heart was his forever when he spoke those words. How could it not be?

That night we kissed and more. We went as far as we could go without things getting out of hand, and while I wanted to, I knew it wasn't time. There were a lot of things I didn't know about being with a boy. Or being with Colton. It

Puddle Jumping

was a learning experience and I was okay with figuring it out and waiting.

After a while, we slowed down and I had to push away, wanting air and needing space so I could collect myself.

"I have to go before your parents get up so we don't get in trouble . . . for this . . ."

"I understand."

He might have, but my heart didn't. It wanted to stay with him.

"I'll see you later," I said. And then, before I could stop myself, I leaned over and gave him one more kiss. "Email me when you get up. We can talk. Like you do with Talia."

He smiled against my cheek and kissed me again. "Talking with you would be much more enjoyable than talking with Talia, Lilly." His eyes scanned the floor by my feet. "She's paint by number; you're a watercolor."

Things like that, moments like those, how do you explain to other people that no one else in the world can you make you feel this way?

chapter eleven

There's a lot to be said about dating Colton. He's smart and interesting and full of important facts and information. He's focused and reliable. He listens. I learn when I'm with him. He sees things around us so differently and he makes me think.

I've always heard your best match in life is the person who is the opposite of you that makes a complete whole. If that's the case, then we were made for each other. My need to be spontaneous and scratch the itch to do dangerous things outweighed a lot of my ability to make responsible decisions.

His mom said she wanted him to have an authentic teenage experience – though I doubt she wanted things to progress in an unhealthy way. I wasn't going to take him to concerts all night and not bring him home until the sun came up. I don't drink. I'm not a rule-breaker in the true sense. But being with someone who doesn't vocalize his affections made it that more important to express ourselves in other ways. I won't go into it, but if I've learned one thing over this year, it's that some things between a boy and a girl are very, very normal.

I wasn't going to let some doctor's opinion of my boyfriend stop me from having the kind of relationship we both deserved. It would be a learning experience and there are things that are slightly different in approach and practice. But I'm always up for a challenge. Especially when it's with him. Or for him. Because it always comes back to him.

* * *

As the weather turned colder, I couldn't go and see him at night. I originally didn't have a hard time getting up the lattice and into the window, but once it started to ice and snow and freeze over, I couldn't justify breaking my neck to get alone time with my boyfriend. Stupid winter.

Our parents began to spend more time together and eventually our mothers were inseparable. Their blooming friendship meant that I got to see my boyfriend more than I would have otherwise. And no one ever said anything when

Puddle Jumping

we would claim to be going upstairs to watch a movie or whatever excuse we made at the time to get away from the boredom that parents bring. Especially when all we wanted to do was go anywhere else and suck face for a few hours.

Which we totally did.

Repeatedly.

When winter break came, my parents decided they were going to leave town to go see my grandparents. But I *really* didn't want to go. The thought of being away from my boyfriend during our first Christmas made me anxious and it did the same for him. It was decided I could stay at his house over the holiday. I thought the adults around us were oblivious to the goings on behind closed doors and we had been stealthy enough to pull the wool over their eyes, but the night I brought all of my stuff over to the Neely's place, I found out I was sorely mistaken.

Sheila and Rick made sure I had everything I needed in the guest room and then Rick had kind of given his wife this . . . *look* . . . and I got a feeling in my stomach like I was in trouble or that perhaps they knew something I didn't.

It's at times like those that your mind quickly goes through worst-case scenarios back to back in your brain. I thought maybe Colton wanted to break up with me, but couldn't say it. Or maybe he had a terminal illness and I would have to marry him like that stupid book they made into a movie with Mandy Moore in it.

I mean, I would definitely marry him at seventeen, if that were the case.

Instead, it was much worse than a terminal illness.

Much, much worse.

Sheila Neely wanted to talk about sex.

The majority of the conversation was lost due to the sound of rushing blood in my ears and humiliation in my brain. I can't remember word for word what was said, but they knew we'd been fooling around. She never came out and said she had heard us but she mentioned something about an increase in dirty laundry and a towel or something. I'm not a hundred percent sure. It was mortifying, though.

I assured her I was a virgin. That Colton was a virgin. And she laughed and said she knew that much, but she wanted to make sure I was okay.

And that made me fall in love with her at the same time I wanted to fall into a hole and disappear forever.

Amber L. Johnson

She wanted nothing more than for her son to have as many predictable teenage experiences as possible. Even if it meant he was groping his girlfriend in her house. I probably should have thanked her or something but my inability to form words was back in full force, and by the time she left the room, I curled up on the guest bed and went fetal, wondering if I could pretend to be in a coma for three months until spring finally came.

Instead, Colton knocked on my door, giving me that disarming smile of his that made me lose all coherent thought. It made the embarrassing conversation with his mom worth it.

That night we celebrated Christmas Eve with his family; mostly with me avoiding eye contact with his mom for fear I would just die on the spot. When everyone was ready to go to bed, he and I walked up the stairs together, hand in hand before he steered me toward his studio instead of escorting me to the guest room.

"I want to give you your present privately, if that's all right with you." He looked shy and . . . come on . . . I'm a girl. Like I was gonna say no?

"Then you get yours, too." It seemed only fair. And I guess as long as I was willing to take his gift early then he was willing to take mine as well. I ran back to the room to get the wrapped box and held it out to him like the proudest girlfriend in the world.

On my insistence, he opened mine first and I was pleasantly surprised he seemed to like what I had given him. I bought him new brushes. They were these freakishly expensive ones he had goo-goo eyes over all the time. He looked at them online like other guys would look at porn. Seriously. Sometimes I wondered if he wanted to feel up those brushes more than me.

He didn't.

But nothing compared to his gift for me. It was leaning in the back of the room, covered in a tarp. A medium sized canvas, transformed with vibrant colors that practically stepped off the painting and onto the floor.

It was of us.

He had painted the two of us staring into one another's faces. Frozen for all of eternity at seventeen and eighteen years old. Perfect and beautiful. Hands holding hands. Eyes staring lovingly into eyes.

It was, as far as I could tell, his way of showing me how he saw us.

66

Puddle Jumping

His way of expressing his adoration.

And possibly his way of communicating that he loved me.

I didn't cry. It would have been the obvious reaction but I wanted him to know that it made me happy. So I smiled until my face hurt and hugged him until my arms felt numb. He put his hands in my hair and rested his chin on my head, not letting on once that he minded if I held him too long.

"I take it that you liked it?" It almost sounded like he was chuckling when he said it.

"I more than like it. I love it."

After thanking him one last time, I went to the guest room, trying in vain to fall asleep. The boy had painted a picture of the two of us and I couldn't rest, thinking of his eyes and his face and how incredibly sweet he was without even knowing it. It was probably ten degrees outside, but under the covers in that foreign bed, I was sweating. I was hot and bothered and wishing I could sneak into his room. But I still felt weird about the talk with his mom earlier.

It made me feel like I needed a shower.

I huffed and puffed and rolled around until the comforter was tangled around one of my legs and the other leg was hanging off the mattress, along with an arm that had gone rogue in my fit of unrest.

I thought about writing. I thought about listening to music. I thought about running in place until I couldn't stand anymore.

Just when I had talked myself into just ignoring it, I heard a sound at the door. It was like one of those horror movies where the doorknob jiggles just a bit, enough to get your attention. I was freaking out thinking about that weird movie where the crazy guy dressed like Santa comes in and slaughters everyone on Christmas Eve . . .

But the door opened and I could see it was, in fact, not a psychotic Santa.

It was Colton.

In just his pajama pants again.

I knew without a doubt what he was there for. But he was sneaking in to see *me* that time, which made it a thousand times better.

"I wanted to see you," he whispered.

There wasn't any hesitation as I shifted the covers and slid my back against the headboard, inviting him in. He simply crawled under the comforter, his skin feeling chilly from the

67

walk down the hall compared to the blazing inferno I had going on between the sheets. His hands on my face gave my arms chill bumps and I was acutely aware of how my body was reacting.

I whispered hello and he smiled in the limited lighting, his fingers sweeping across my shoulder like he was memorizing every inch with his fingertips. Over the tree branches branded into my skin and lower to graze my fingers. I didn't flinch when he touched me. I welcomed it.

I told him again I loved his present and he kissed the side of my mouth in response.

"I hoped that it was an appropriate Christmas gift. My mom said she thought you would like it."

"Your mom was right."

"I'll tell her that."

It wasn't too soon for me to tell him I loved him. I knew it wasn't. But I was so damn afraid, you see. Because I wasn't sure how that worked with him.

Instead, I kissed him as softly as I could, hoping he would feel it there instead of me saying it.

Things heated up pretty quickly and soon we were wrapped around each other. We were pros at it by then. Touching. Kissing. Exploring without hesitation. By then almost all of our clothes were off, and even though we'd mostly just done a little stuff and kissed, it almost happened. Because kissing can lead to touching and touching can lead to shorts being tugged and then you're right there and you're almost doing it. IT. *The* IT.

Not to be confused with The It I was touching while we were naked.

It was the first time we'd been that way. The first time we'd actually put our hands on anything other than over the shirt and pants and stuff.

So I, once again, had to stop it from going further than we were ready for. I mean, I don't know if he was ready or not. I wasn't. It was when *he* realized we'd been so close to doing something major that he jumped off the bed, his eyes wide and hands in his hair again before he bee-lined for the bathroom.

I think a cuddle would have been better than falling off the mattress as he slammed the bathroom door.

But it is what it is.

Puddle Jumping

chapter  twelve

We stayed in separate rooms that night. I figured maybe it would be best to have our space. He seemed to agree. It was easy between me and Colton when it came to things like that.

Opening presents with his mom and dad wasn't nearly as awkward as I thought it would be. And their gift to me made me blush and smile because I knew what it was for. They had purchased two tickets to the Museum of Art in downtown Philly. All access, or whatever they were. Year round. Every exhibit.

One part of me was thrilled.

Another part of me gave Mrs. Neely the side eye because I thought maybe she was relieved not to have to go all the time herself.

Though, I'm sure after years of listening to the same facts about painters, it could have gotten a little old for her.

Not me, though. Everything about Colton was magical and I wanted as much time as possible to soak him up.

My parents returned that evening and I left Colton's house feeling lighter than air. As soon as I got there, our painting went up on my wall.

Due to what had happened in the guest room Christmas Eve, I had a brief thought that maybe I needed to talk to someone about birth control. Because if we had gotten that close as fast as we did, who knew if the actual thing would happen if we got carried away.

I tried to get the courage up to talk with my mom about getting put on the pill.

Once.

Twice.

Three times.

By the fourth time I started to open my mouth to ask, I got so flustered I just ended up leaving room and I swear I heard my dad say something about 'freaky teenage girl hormones'.

He had *no effing idea.*

Puddle Jumping

I went to Harper. And Marissa. Even Quinn. Because, with as cool as Mrs. Neely had been about sticky towels and things, I wasn't about to ask her about condoms.

Harper was predictable, wanting to know about the experience itself but I was embarrassed to tell her I wasn't prepared for the actual act because touching him had freaked me out. Why had she never told me that the skin *moved*?

She should have told me that, at least.

Marissa was way more helpful.

"Wait. You said he won't wear gloves on his hands because of his 'sensory' issues, right?"

"Yeah. So?"

She shook her head like I was as shallow as they came. "So, if he won't wear rubber gloves on his hands, what makes you think he'll wear one *there*?"

Why the hell didn't I think of that? He was my boyfriend. I knew enough about his 'specific nature' that condoms, much like gloves and balloons, were probably not going to be something he would touch, or allow to touch him. Especially in that very sensitive . . . region.

I was screwed without being screwed. A virgin looking for birth control for sex that wasn't going to happen yet.

Inevitably, I had to go to Quinn. She had some hook-ups at the Planned Parenthood office and she also did some volunteer work at the hospital twice a month. I guess . . . she never really said . . . but I think she stole samples. She had essentially taken a year's worth from the hospital, handing them over to me like it was no big deal. I just needed to remember to take them every day.

I noticed weird things within the first month. My skin looked amazing. Also, I was a cranky, crazy bitch. Like being a teenage girl wasn't bad enough. Lastly, my boobs were huge.

No joke. My bunny slopes turned into Mount Vesuvius practically overnight. I had to buy new bras but used the excuse my old ones were just ratty. My mom never even asked. I just told her up front they were gross so she wouldn't pry.

Colton certainly didn't seem to mind the changes in my body. In fact, he would become so engrossed in my chest I would have to steer him in another direction to be able to proceed with anything else.

We spent a lot of time studying and my GPA went up a whole point. So did Harper's. I guess it rubbed off on her, too. But I think it freaked her out because she was used to being the pretty girl and the easy girl, but she never thought about being the smart girl.

In time, she started to see herself as more than a pair of boobs in heels and I think hanging out with our group of friends made her a little more discerning with the guys she hooked up with.

Well, that and one of the girls on the Pep Squad got Chlamydia on her cheek because she laid the wrong way in a tanning bed and everyone started rumors about Chlam-eyes and Chlam-face. So who knew how many degrees of separation there were and if you'd somehow end up with it, too?

* * *

I worried about graduation. Because Colton was so much more acclimated at that point, and having to start something new could have been harder on him than most. It was only a few months before he was supposed to turn eighteen, and he'd already started to blend in more, while still standing out for being gorgeous and smarter than most of our classmates thanks to his tutors and his focus.

I found that, while Colton couldn't always catch on to my attitudes through body language or certain phrases, much less sighs and annoyed huffs, he could pretty much get what kind of mood I was in by paying attention to the music I would listen to. It was just another way we could communicate without talking about stuff, because, well, we're teenagers and terrible communicators to begin with which only meant another hurdle to overcome.

On the drive to school, I could play certain songs and he would perceive I was in a good mood or a cranky one. The good ones were always from him, so he never had to worry about that. But he was always a little unsure of what to say or do if I was upset about something. School. My parents. Homework. A little fight with Harper. He found it strange, like whatever was making me irritated or moody was just unnecessary. Sometimes it helped to put things into perspective. Sometimes it made my head hurt. Sometimes I would get exasperated over it all.

But then I would talk to my other friends and I realized that pretty much all boys are like that. None of them really get why girls are upset over petty and stupid drama, so it made me feel like maybe our relationship was as ordinary as they came.

That was, until that horrible day in February.

You know which one I'm referring to.

Puddle Jumping

That one.

I loathe it.

I think Valentine's Day is when my cynicism started to rear its ugly little head.

V-Day. Heart Day. Love Day. St. Valentine's Day.

Don't those two words alone just make you want to cut a bitch? Like, as if it's not bad enough the mascot for the day is a baby in a diaper with wings and a weapon . . . it's a day when the entire universe is pretty much required to purchase pink and red Dollar Store gifts and proclaim their love for everyone . . . everywhere. So, that morning I was playing some angsty girl rock when I went to pick Colton up because I just knew school was going to be an explosion of flowers and candy and I was going to be the Valentine's Day Gretchen Wieners, sitting in class while Glen Coco got sugar cookies and carnations handed to him, and I didn't.

My old boyfriend hadn't made a big deal last year, but we had exchanged cards. It just wasn't the same because I was actually in love with Colton.

I'm not the girl who falls in love and gets excited over girly things and wants flowers or public declarations of love. But . . . maybe with Colton I did want those things.

Because I thought I couldn't have them.

I was bracing myself for it.

Imagine how surprised and guilty I felt when I knocked on his front door that morning and he met me with a bouquet of wildflowers. Pink . . . blue . . . purple . . . held tightly in his fist and pretty much pushed into my face as soon as I walked into the foyer.

"These are for you."

I mean, it was obvious Mrs. Neely had purchased them. Colton looked like he had no idea why he was handing them over to me anyway. Wooing and courting were my area, not his, so I didn't take any offense. As girls, we always have these ridiculous expectations anyway. It's no wonder guys are so confused all the time.

Sheila hugged me and wished me Happy Valentine's Day before presenting me with a red envelope that held dinner reservations at Taste, this super upscale restaurant downtown inside of the museum. I knew it would probably mean we would get the food to go, but the thought was still there. The heart . . . Mrs. Neely's heart . . . was still there in the gift.

She tried so hard to overcompensate for what Colton didn't get. As did I.

We bent and bent and bent until we were pretzels because we loved him.

"Dinner at six," she whispered and gave me a smile. "You're welcome to come back here and watch a movie if you'd like. Rick and I will be going to dinner, too, but our reservations aren't until eight or so. We'll be home late."

And there it was. Like she was telling me, without telling me, that we would have the house to ourselves for a while.

But that she would definitely be coming back.

Mrs. Neely was the coolest mom on the planet.

I thanked her and she kept the flowers for me to pick up later in the evening and, suddenly, I was really, *really* into the Valentine's Day spirit.

Colton smiled from the passenger seat and took my hand as he always did. "Are you happy with the dinner tonight?"

"I am."

"And you liked the flowers."

"I did."

He nodded and leaned back to relax a little in the seat. "Will you stay over?"

I laughed a little and squeezed his hand. "I'm not sure your mom would be okay with that. But I'll definitely stay for a while."

"I'd like that."

My parents had been good about me spending the night with Colton over Christmas, but this would be a whole separate issue that I wasn't willing to push.

Valentine's Day was rapidly becoming my very favorite day of the year. And I was pretty sure I wanted to finally go all the way with him that night.

In the span of a day, all of it had been decided. It was going to happen.

I raced home from school, stopping just long enough to drop Colton off at his house with a quick kiss before rushing to my room to grab my clothes, leaving a note for my parents that I had dinner plans, then hauling ass to Harper's to get ready. I was a sweaty mess, full of nerves and excitement, only half listening to her as she talked me through it all. She was giving me weird pointers and telling me things I couldn't comprehend because I'm more of a visual person and some of the stuff she was describing sounded like they couldn't physically be accomplished with gravity working against us.

By the time she was done with me I looked . . . well, I looked really, really pretty.

Puddle Jumping

Harper gave me a hug, smacked me on the ass and sent me on my way, yelling "Good luck!" as I drove off.

In my head, I was moving toward my destiny.

But the best laid plans of mice and men often go awry, as I would find out firsthand.

Colton looked amazing, so that wasn't an issue.

I was in a dress for God's sake. That wasn't the problem.

We enjoyed the ride down to the museum together, listening to music and holding hands. I'd ask questions and he'd respond. We talked. In my mind, I kept trying to plan out exactly how things would go for the rest of the evening. But that was probably where it started to unravel. Anything my mind could have come up with would not have been what Colton would have been thinking as soon as we cleared the doors to the museum.

We arrived early enough to start our walk through the exhibits, milling through the larger than usual crowds. Because, apparently, other people thought looking at art on Stupid Cupid's Day was fun, too. Of course, they were pretty much old people. Like, at least thirty-five or older, and they were drinking and conversing, causing more noise than usual.

It didn't bother me, of course. I was with him. And nothing ever mattered when we were together except each other.

Ask me anything about art. Impressionism. Surrealism. Contemporary. Avant-Garde. I'm pretty sure I could tell you enough to warrant an eye roll and cause you to mutter that I'm a snobby know-it-all. But I paid attention to what Colton talked about. I tried to see as clearly as he did the things that fascinated him. And at times, he could become so focused it was as if I were blending into the background instead of being by his side, but I didn't care.

Because the only thing I was that passionate about . . . was him.

You call it obsessive, I call it being devoted.

We walked for a bit and discussed certain pieces, until someone recognized him. See, being in a museum with a locally famous artist, you don't always get to lay low. And with the amount of people around that night, I was surprised he hadn't been accosted earlier. That knowledge did nothing to ease my frustration when the time came for our reservation and Colton was still talking art to a handful of adults who were hanging on his every word.

I tried to interrupt but there was no real way to do it. Eventually, I had to step in front of him, feeling stupid and small, unimportant and immature as I relayed I would go to the restaurant alone and wait for him. Which is exactly what I did. And as I waited and waited and waited at the table for him to arrive, I realized I was having Valentine's dinner . . . by myself.

It hurt. A lot. But I didn't want to be the girl who cried into her overpriced pasta.

No. Not me.

Instead, I counted all of the good things we had. I tried to envision what the rest of the night would be like. Unfortunately, after half an hour, I knew it would be no use to wait any longer – and the waitress said she might need the table, so I ordered his food to go and walked it to the car myself before going back inside the museum to find him.

He was in the exact same spot. Alone now. Staring at one of three pieces from the Van Gogh exhibit: Starry Night.

"I was looking for you." I tried not to sound upset, and hoped I had succeeded.

Finally, he acknowledged me. "I've read this was Van Gogh's way of portraying hope. Hope from escaping his hell on earth; being trapped in his body as it began to recede. An escape from his mind as he stayed in an asylum. Those clouds . . . they're representations of freedom. Heaven. A cure for his illness."

His fingers rose to point.

"The brush strokes are impeccable. The majority of the print is from memories of his childhood."

I just stood as still as possible, taking in the meaning behind of each of his words.

"And what would you paint from your childhood?" I asked, simply a whisper, forgetting about being put-out from dinner, and now completely entranced by him.

He looked over at me with that smile. Slight. Meaningful.

"You."

Puddle Jumping

chapter thirteen

Blood rushed up to my face and I gripped his hand in mine, asking him quietly if we could go back to his house. I felt alive . . . so freaking alive and excited to get back to his place. I didn't care about anything that had just happened. Just like that.

The night was chilly, but clear, and I vividly remember looking up at the stars, my chest swelling and filling up to the point of almost bursting because I loved him so much. I loved him with a physical ache in my chest.

Love? Sometimes it's so big it hurts.

Once back at the house, I put the food in to reheat because I figured we would need the energy for what I had planned later on. And while we waited, I skimmed his channels for a movie to watch or order. Settling on one that looked romantic in an odd way, I set it up and plated the food, making us a little picnic on the floor. My bouquet was sitting right off to the side of us and I liked the way it felt. It was just right.

But the movie? The movie was probably the second worst thing of the night.

I honestly had no idea what it was about. I'd barely heard of it and none of my friends had ever said anything about seeing it. How was I supposed to know?

It wasn't until we were halfway through finishing our food that it dawned on me that the lead character had Asperger's.

By then Colton was fascinated, his attention fixated on the movie, his brow creased as he watched. I was swept away in the female lead's part of the story. At times she was cold, and at times she was irritated. But I saw a lot of myself in her, and it was . . . odd. Our food went cold and neither of us spoke as the film progressed, but I could feel the tension in the room begin to rise.

"I can turn it off . . ." I started but Colton just shook his head, transfixed.

"I'd like to finish it."

Puddle Jumping

I felt like I was holding my breath the entire time and pushing back tears because these people were older . . . and . . . there was no Hollywood ending. Just reality. The reality of loving someone who may never, ever be able to love you back in the same capacity.

But Colton could, right? We were different. We had to be. He could explain things so clearly and show his affections in other ways and there was nothing that would make me ever quit loving him. I was sure of it.

The credits rolled and I sat in stunned silence, because there wasn't a happy ending.

There was no happy ending.

None.

I needed that happy ending.

The silence was overwhelming as I cleaned up the dishes and loaded the washer.

"I'm going to get ready for bed." Colton disappeared to his room to start his routine and I debated on whether or not to follow.

What we'd just watched reverberated through my mind.

I didn't want that for us.

I couldn't allow myself to wallow in those thoughts. Instead, I focused on getting up the stairs to his room. He was in the shower when I got there and for a moment, I paused.

Until he called my name.

"Lilly?"

"Yeah, I'm here." I walked into the bathroom and sat on the toilet seat, overcome by thoughts and emotions and unable to think clearly.

"Will you join me?"

The shower curtain moved back slightly as his head poked out, water running down his face and dripping from his chin as he gazed at me sitting there. As much as he could be concerned, he looked like he was, and I hated to see him that way. Something in the way he was looking at me pulled at my heart and every last expectation I had for the night flew out the window.

"Are you upset? Did you not like dinner?"

"I liked dinner," I said quietly. I couldn't say what I was upset about. It felt too much like folding.

Instead of stripping and getting into ridiculous lingerie to seduce him, I stood, pulled off my dress, and stepped into the shower, under the warm spray of the water to just . . . hold him. In a watery embrace. So that he couldn't see the difference between the water from above and the tears as they silently flowed.

I didn't even care about possibly having to explain why my hair was wet when his parents got home.

* * *

I'm not a quitter. Not by a long shot.

I mean, if I was a smoker and needed to quit, that would be one thing. But Colton? Never.

Just because two people in a movie couldn't make it work didn't mean we would be like that. I wasn't giving up on us just yet.

Then, the next week, he dropped a new bomb on me: He got a job.

I was more surprised than anyone else.

I'd gone to pick him up from school and Mrs. Neely dropped the bomb on me, explaining the situation and asking if I would mind driving him to work after our last class of the day.

Apparently, on the night of our visit to the museum on Valentine's, Colton had spoken with the curator and there was an internship open that my boyfriend agreed to. Just like that. On the spot. His PEERS teacher had been talking about jobs and Colton didn't see a problem with it. It was exactly what he loved to do.

Of course, he talked it over with his parents, but not with me. And I hated that, but there was nothing I could do about it. It's not that he didn't care or didn't think of me. I am of the opinion that he had always discussed things with them and that was how it went. He respected his parents and they were the final word over every decision he'd ever made.

I didn't think driving him to and from work would be something my parents would be okay with. Going in and out of the city that much wouldn't sit well with my dad.

In the end, it wasn't going to work out for me to do it, so Mrs. Neely started picking him up every day after school. That meant we had less time together, one-on-one, because the few minutes we had in the car to and from school had always been our special time. And lunch didn't count. Neither did English. I wanted *to be alone with him.*

After he started his internship, we only saw each other in the morning on the drive there and at our lockers. By the time he got home at night, with his new schedule, he was finding it hard to adapt to the changes in his routine and I learned very quickly I needed to stop pushing the issue. He was getting irritable more easily and instead of letting my feelings get hurt, I did something entirely different.

I started babysitting again.

I'm not sure why I did it, really. Maybe not being able to see Colton as much was making me feel lonely. Maybe I just needed to prove to myself that I could find an interest in other things outside of him. My mom had made remarks a few times that maybe I should spend more time with my other friends or find a hobby. Instead, I chose the job. It was probably stupid to do, but I hadn't babysat the twins much since we'd started dating and it was easy money after school.

It gave me time to clear my head when I got anxious about our relationship. I knew every morning I would get to see him. We just had to bide our time until then. Being busy helped the time go faster. Phone calls to friends worked, but hanging out with a couple only made me miss him more.

He'd made friends with a few other interns and would speak of them from time to time, but we'd never met because he was so busy. The additional socialization added extra stress to his already full schedule of art and school, along with his PEERS classes and me. But I was seeing some changes in him for the better and it made all of it seem worth it.

He started watching people more closely, and I could tell he was trying out certain mannerisms or phrases the other interns probably used. While I had been the catalyst for his journey to become more social, at least according to his mom, the internship was what *really* brought him out of his shell. Maybe it was because the other interns were guys, as well. Or maybe it was because he got to talk art all day: eat it, breathe it, live it.

Whatever it was, I was glad. No matter how much I missed him. This was what I wanted from day one.

We still emailed when we could. We still saw each other as much as possible. But the extreme difference from the initial time we'd been together, seemingly glued at the hip, to the sporadic moments we got at that time, was a difficult transition.

For me.

If it was hard for him to be away from me, I wouldn't have known. He fell into his groove and just went with it like it was just a natural progression.

Our physical relationship slowed down a bit, since we hardly had private time together except in the car. There were a few days where we'd been driving to school and his hand would wander up my leg and I'd have to debate on whether or not to skip first period just to get some interaction him. I certainly didn't want the school calling his parents about him being tardy or absent, but . . . dammit. I *missed* him.

For a while my conscience won me over and I was proud I decided to keep driving until we got to the school where we would kiss for a few minutes before heading to our lockers. But . . . I wasn't always so strong. In fact, I started picking him up a few minutes early sometimes; just to give us the option of finding a side road to park on.

I had no idea how much I craved his touch. How much just hearing his voice, no matter how limited his words. He'd become everything to me so quickly I hadn't had time to see it happening until I was too far gone.

I was so far gone. I had no idea.

The week before prom, I'd been up to my eyeballs in *everything*. I was busy getting my dress and things ready, along with schoolwork and trying to keep up with my friends and my boyfriend. I'm sure I was spaced out more than usual, and the ride to school with him by my side was probably quieter than we'd become used to. But I had so much on my mind; I didn't think anything of it.

We were on our way to school, passing by one of the few side roads we'd claimed as our own when our need to be with one another was way too much to ignore, when I started up a conversation.

"Are your friends at the museum going to prom with their girlfriends?"

Colton's hand was squeezing mine a little tighter than usual before I felt him shift in his seat and he spoke loudly into the quiet car. Placing our hands on my lap, he asked the most heart obliterating question I'd ever heard. "Lilly, would you enjoy it if we..."

I'm not going to repeat it here. But you probably get the gist. It's pretty much third base. Okay, it's almost a home run.

The car fishtailed from my foot hitting the brake so hard and unexpectedly. I slammed into the steering wheel, hitting the shit out of my sore boobs and stared at him like Bambi watching his mom getting killed.

"What?" I'm pretty sure that was my eloquent response. "I mean we're already pretty . . . physical." I knew what we had and had not done and it shouldn't have surprised me that he was suggesting it, but to hear him say it was a completely different beast all together.

Puddle Jumping

He straightened in the seat and looked at me for a moment. "Justin and Keith talk a lot about their girlfriends and the things they do. . ." Then he went on a very clinical diatribe about my lady business and what they suggested that he do to it. And also what they liked their girlfriends to do to them.

"Yeah, no. I get what you're saying." I tried to stop him with my hand up as I attempted to keep from laughing, and dying, at the same time. I drove for a bit, considering my next sentence carefully. Pulling to a stop on a desolate stretch of wooded gravel road, I killed the engine and turned in my seat to appraise him.

We were definitely going to be late that morning.

We'd never really talked much about that part of our relationship - it had just happened organically, but I guess hearing about it from two people he would consider 'neurotypical' had made him focus on it a lot. *A lot a lot.*

"Is it something you'd like to do?"

His eyes were looking out the window as he thought. "I've seen things before. I'm not entirely sure what the point is, though."

So he'd been watching videos.

See? Just like a regular guy after all.

"I guess it's because it feels good. Like when I touch you while we kiss."

Sly smile. Of course it did.

"It's not really necessary, you know. It's not something people *have* to do to show their affections."

At the time, I had no idea why I was trying to talk him out of it.

Maybe I secretly knew.

"Colton?"

He looked at me with those eyes, and his lips were so soft looking, and his face was so confused.

"Would you . . . would you like to? I mean, we don't have to."

I loved him. I wanted to. But only if *he* wanted to.

He had to want to. Not because of any other reason than it was his decision.

It was hesitant, his yes. His looked unsure and I'll be honest, so was I.

"Yes."

"Yes?"

"Yes."

And then my anxiety kicked in.

83

Amber L. Johnson

What if it was a bad move?

I could be so, so, *so* bad at it.

I was panicking.

He just took a few moments to accept his answer and after a couple deep breaths he looked into my eyes for a second. Then he nodded and we were quiet as we moved from the front seat to the back.

I was intimidated a little.

Okay, a lot.

"Just tell me if it's too much, or if it doesn't feel good, okay?"

I knew he would be honest. That wasn't an issue. The issue was that I'd never done it before.

I took my time but he was shaking, his eyes half closed and lips trembling slightly below reddened cheeks. His chest rose and fell in erratic rhythms and I braced myself for him to ask me to stop. But he didn't.

After a few minutes I got worried and looked up again to see his face scrunched up anxiously. So I stopped.

"Should I do something different?"

He closed his eyes and brought his fists to his forehead in distress. "Too much," he breathed. "I can't . . . I can't . . ." And that was about the time he started to get upset. I hadn't seen him freak out about much before, except for Christmas Eve, but this seemed larger. He choked out words about the way it felt and how his body was reacting, that it felt good but it didn't and it wasn't the same as any of the other stuff we did.

"It's okay," I told him, pushing aside the feelings I was having at listening to him. "We can stop. We don't have to." I promised him.

The truth was that I felt like a failure.

But it wasn't about me.

He was becoming increasingly agitated, shaking his head back and forth, squeezing his eyes shut and pushing his fists into the roof of the car. The words coming out of his mouth were all over the place but I could understand what he was conveying was that he just wanted to do the same stuff everyone else could and he was frustrated that it was so hard for us.

"It's not this difficult for other people." His eyes were open and staring out the window, his hands pressed against the ceiling as he breathed heavily.

Puddle Jumping

"So what? So what if other people do this stuff? I don't care." I was reaching for his face and fighting back the tears threatening to show themselves again. Because he had tears in his eyes, too. "I don't care what other people do. Because none of those other people are you."

He closed his eyes.

"I only want you, no matter what, okay? Only you and me. The rest doesn't matter."

It was true. With everything he and I had experienced physically, I couldn't say doing that particular activity would be a deal breaker. He had so much more to offer than just that.

I crawled into his lap and wrapped my legs around his sides, tucking my arms behind his head and pressing my forehead to his. There was about a minute of silence before he stopped shaking. Before his hands rested against the outside of my legs and he pressed them harder to his body. I flexed my thigh muscles and squeezed them against his hips, listening as a rush of air escaped his lungs.

And then, slowly, he opened his eyes. "That makes the noise disappear."

"Yeah? When I squeeze you like this?" I did it again.

He nodded, letting his lids close.

"I'll remember that," I whispered, kissing him firmly on the forehead.

His hands started to roam up my back and under my shirt and he breathed out long and slow. "You're my quiet, Lilly."

Shaking my head, I mumbled, "I'm the one who got you worked up in the first place."

His fingers traced the sides of my waist. "For as long as I can remember, you've been the one to calm me down."

"How's that even possible? When we were kids, I almost died every time we were together. I'm a mess. I'm chaos."

"No," he whispered. "You're my beautiful Lilly. The one who makes everything right in my world."

That day I felt like we saw each other in exactly the same way.

Amber L. Johnson

chapter fourteen

Then there was prom.

I watched a movie once where the lead actor said prom was an important rite of passage for teenagers. That it shouldn't be missed. And I guess that's a pretty true statement because I've heard of ladies who missed going to theirs and it scarred them for life. Like, they ended up being crazy and losing their minds, writing their memoirs from behind bars and linking it all back to the night they missed their prom.

Seriously. Watch an episode of *Snapped*.

Anyway, with as much as it was supposedly this big deal, I wasn't quite sure I agreed. It was just another dance with people from school. Except, the dresses were more expensive and it was being held in a hotel instead of in the gym.

I think we put a lot of pressure on ourselves to be excited about these things. That they're defining moments we *cannot* miss out on because they're once in a lifetime. While I think memories are good to have, the buildup is usually better than the actual event.

Maybe if we stopped trying to achieve movie standards of greatness, we'd be happy with what we have.

I wish I'd had that mindset for prom when it came around. I should have expected it wouldn't turn out the way I'd hoped.

* * *

My dress was white, much to my dad's annoyance. He kept eyeing me like I had chosen a damn wedding dress and I had to roll my eyes an infinite number of times before he finally stopped gawking. I'd gone all out and had actually worn my hair up . . . I guess I really wanted to feel like I looked pretty that night.

Sue. Me. I'm still a girl.

Anyway, I'd been getting ready up in my room with Harper when the first phone call came in. It was Mrs. Neely and she sounded really apologetic, but Colton was still at work doing something for one of the exhibits, so he was staying late to try and get it finished.

And, as I knew, Colton usually completed any project he was given.

"When do you think he'll be done?" I was holding the phone against my ear while trying to do my blush and failing miserably.

She didn't know but promised to call me as soon as she did because she was going to try to tell him one more time how important his promise was to me. And that work could wait.

Mrs. Neely had a *tone*.

Disappointment set in as soon as I disconnected and my best friend tried her hardest to make me feel better by just being . . . well . . . Harper. She was cracking jokes and making stupid faces and voices to get my mind off it, but there was no denying it would be Valentine's Day all over again and I would be in the limo by myself that night. Alone at dinner.

By myself at the dance.

I took pictures with the group, not as a couple.

I had no corsage.

The hardest thing was watching everyone else with their dates; matchy-matchy and all goo-goo eyed at one another. It just drove the point in even more I was alone that night.

Quinn and Sawyer with her pink dress and his pink vest.

Harper in her yellow dress . . . with two dates.

I suppose it was lucky for me that she had two: Blake and Derek. Laugh all you want, but neither of the guys cared they were both taking her to the dance. I'm pretty sure she'd promised them something I didn't want to know about.

After all of the progress she had made . . .

They were nice. Attractive. Pleasant. She was happy. I couldn't say anything to her about it. Tigers don't change their stripes, as my mom would say. Or is that zebras?

The theme of the dance was James Bond or something equivalent. Pictures were being taken as soon as you went through the door, and I was super bummed with the thought of having to walk in alone, having a picture taken by myself when I actually, truly, did have a boyfriend. He just wasn't there.

But before I could step foot into the massive ballroom, Harper stopped me and pulled me aside to tell me Blake would walk me in, if I wanted him to. It didn't really matter. It wasn't like I was going to buy one of the photos. I just didn't want

Puddle Jumping

that pity look people were so quick to give. And the photographer was stopping everyone from taking group pictures at the door, so, really, what choice did I have?

Blake was tall and tan, with kind of a little faux-hawk on top of his head. I wondered if he had a tattoo . . . a piercing or something equally as exotic as his Hawaiian roots. I wondered exactly how old he was, because he had a baby face but this really sick looking manly body. He probably worked out five times a week. There was a seventy - thirty chance that he was in his mid-twenties.

He had an easy smile and reminded me of one of those guys who winks after they say something they think you will think is cute. I thanked him for taking pity on me and linked my arm through his, stopping in front of the photographer to give a half-hearted smile before we stepped through the door and into the frenzy of bouncing bodies who just the day before had resembled people I went to school with.

Now half of the girls looked like pageant queens and the other half looked like hookers.

I wondered which one I resembled.

Blake had no problem offering me pity dances and getting me a drink here and there. As it was, I was trying to have fun, no matter how hollow my chest felt.

Prom King and Queen were announced and I got choked up when Quinn and Sawyer won, taking their crowns and kissing each other in front of the entire student body. It meant something. It just . . . *did*. Regardless of who they were in a classroom, they were Quinn and Sawyer. Everyone knew them. They were equal opportunity in every last way.

After they had their dance, Harper pulled me to the side to tell me she was headed out front for a smoke with Blake. Derek had made a friend or two at the table where we'd stashed all our stuff and I had to laugh that he was chatting up a snobby cheerleader named Claire. *The* Claire of Chlam-Face fame.

I went outside with Harper because I had nothing better to do and I figured it could help clear my head a little. I'll be honest, I was straight up *moping*.

She and Blake stood off to the side of the hotel, down an alley, smoking cigarettes and kissing and I felt like a third wheel, but it looked like that was the theme of the evening anyway. It was colder than I expected and I hadn't brought a jacket, so I was doing that weird self-hug, watching the way the wind was making my dress whip around my feet. That's why I didn't notice Blake approaching me and hanging his jacket over my arms. I didn't notice until I looked up and he was squinting away from the smoke coming out of the cigarette hanging from his lips as he put it on my shoulders.

I told him thanks and he smiled, taking the cig in his fingers and tapping it. I remember watching the way the ashes dipped and lifted in the wind. It was a little poetic, in a way. If you're into that kind of stuff.

Harper was on the cell with her mom, so he and I were chatting, listening as the music from the dance bled through every crack in the building. It was so loud. *So damn loud.*

And maybe that was why I wasn't paying attention to my phone in my little clutch.

Or maybe it was how loud the wind was in my ears and that's why I didn't hear anyone calling my name from the street.

Why I didn't hear footsteps.

Perhaps it was why I didn't give any thought to how close I was to Blake or how his hands were rubbing my arms up and down in an attempt to warm me as we waited for his date to get off the phone.

Nope.

I didn't hear any of that.

But I did see Colton's fist before it collided with Blake's jaw.

In retrospect, I should have known that Colton seeing me with another guy would set him off. But I hadn't heard Sheila call. I didn't know Colton had changed clothes at work and his intern friend Keith was walking him to meet me. I didn't know any of that. All I knew was I was at my prom with my limited amount of friends, waiting for my boyfriend who appeared out of nowhere to defend me for no reason whatsoever.

The fallout was quick, with Colton jumping on Blake and throwing him to the ground, while Blake tried to push him off, shouting profanities and me yelling for them both to stop and trying to explain Colton was *different* . . . something I never wanted to say before in my entire life, but Blake had no idea and I hadn't said anything to him about my boyfriend.

Plus, I didn't even know if he was going to show!

They rolled around on the concrete until Blake got the dominant position, pinning Colton beneath him and folding his arms against his chest while my boyfriend struggled and yelled out words that I'd never heard him use before.

Puddle Jumping

With as embarrassed as I should have been . . . with as angry as it should have made me . . . as much as I know I should have yelled at him and walked away from it all . . . I couldn't

He was my Colton.

The pressure on his chest seemed to give him the squeeze he needed to focus and calm down while I got on my knees, cold concrete and even colder wind chilling me to the bone, to speak into his ear. I explained as factually as I could that Blake was Harper's date and he had lent me his jacket because I was cold.

I wanted to say, 'because *you* weren't here'.

'Because I couldn't have *your* coat'.

'Because you may not have offered it to me . . .'

Instead, I placed my hand firmly on his forehead and whispered for him to look at my face and listen to me.

Blake got carefully off him, stepping back and rubbing his jaw a little. And Harper just looked on like she was partially impressed and partially terrified.

When Colton finally pulled himself to his feet, his suit rumpled and dirty . . . my corsage crushed and falling apart on the ground . . . my dress stained from the sidewalk . . . he had an appropriate look of remorse on his face.

"We walked." He pointed to someone standing off to the side of the scene.

"I brought him over from the museum to make sure he got here." The stranger took a moment before extending his hand to mine. "I'm Keith. I take it you must be Lilly?"

I only nodded.

He looked me over from head to toe and gave a small smile. "I can see why he'd fight for you."

That was the first time I lost patience with our relationship. Not because Colton was who he was . . . is who he is . . . but because it occurred to me if anyone on the outside was looking in and didn't know about us, it looked like Colton was just a bad boyfriend. All of the gentle and sweet things between us were in private. The screw-ups were public. And, maybe I was worn out from being the understanding one, but it really felt like we'd been together long enough to be able to sit down and have a talk about how his actions that night made me feel.

I silently took us to our hotel room, not even bothering to say anything to any of the rest of our friends. Harper knew where we were going and she could relay the message if it needed to be repeated. Colton was quiet, too, and just followed me into the room. No questions asked. It was that type of trust in him that made my heart hurt so badly.

I knew I needed a moment to gather myself, so I went into the bathroom to change into some pajamas, not remembering I had packed yet another stupid little nightie thing instead of regular shorts and a t-shirt. It hardly seemed appropriate, so I opted for the underwear I had packed for the following day and an undershirt, pulling my stupid hair down and practically screaming at the irritating amounts of bobby pins used to keep it in place. My overly hair-sprayed locks went up into a sloppy poof on top of my head and I washed my face of all of the useless make-up I didn't need to face the guy I loved.

When I walked out of the bathroom, he was sitting on the bed. Shoes off. Jacket discarded. Staring at the wall.

He took a deep breath and continued to focus there. "Lilly. Sometimes I don't think I have the capacity to be what you need in a significant other."

"Okay. Well, I feel that way about me sometimes." I was being honest as I crawled across the comforter to sit next to him and stare at the same spot he was.

He shifted on the bed and touched my leg with his fingertips, roaming gently across my kneecap. "I certainly don't feel that way about you. You've always been patient."

I nodded. "Yeah. But it's hard."

His silence let me know he wanted me to explain further.

"Look," I started, guarding my heart as best I could to not burst into tears, "tonight was special to me. And you weren't here."

"I was asked to stay late at work."

I finally chanced a look into his eyes. "But you promised me first. Do you remember that? I specifically asked you if you wanted to go to prom with me and you said yes. You said *yes*, Colton."

If 'realization' actually had a look, it would be the one that flashed across his face at that moment. "I see."

"Do you see?" I shifted to sit and face him. "It was important to me because we haven't seen each other very much lately because of your new job. It was important because we're graduating soon. I wanted us to spend time together with our friends. Because friendship is important."

"Friendship is important to me. You're important to me."

Puddle Jumping

"And *you're* important to *me*. So *very* important. I want to spend any little bit of time I can with you. I subjected myself to dressing up and doing my hair and, just, all of this damn effort . . ." Tears really were stinging my eyes by that point. Until his hand cupped my chin.

"It was unnecessary."

"To you." I looked at his eyes this time. "It was unnecessary to *you*. Not to me. This was important to me. And I need you . . . to make me important. To you."

"You've always been important."

"I've always been important here," finger to his heart, "and here," finger to his head. "But I need to be important all over. Not just when we're alone. Not just when you feel like you have time. I am *just* as important as your job. And you made a promise to me you would be here at prom. I've overlooked other things, but tonight, I need you to understand that my feelings are hurt and I want your promises to me to be just as important as your promises to other people. If you say you're going to do something with me, then do it."

My chest felt tight.

"I understand."

Just like that. It was said, so it must be done. I wasn't forcing him to do anything other than keep his word.

And that's when it happened.

"I love you, Colton. I do. And I want us to be together."

His silence was piercing and my heartbeat in my ears was threatening to make me go deaf. But I had to give him the benefit.

"Don't say it back, okay? I just want you to know that I . . . love you."

Colton's mouth started to open and then closed slowly, his hand taking mine in his as he stared down at it. I closed my eyes and willed my anxiety away, feeling his fingers trace over my skin. A pattern. Soft lines of his fingers playing over the top of my hand.

Like a paint brush stroking my skin.

I didn't need him to say it out loud. He'd told me with his touch. His actions, over his words, solidified what I needed in my heart.

Amber L. Johnson

chapter fifteen

From that point on, Colton did what he said he would do. If we made plans, he kept them. His mom saw to it if it looked like he was going in another direction. And he put me first, which felt amazing. It wasn't forced. I just had to set exact expectations. Say what I meant. Be literal.

We had a new understanding, and it worked.

The last three weeks of school flew by. Between studying for finals and actually taking them, my head was focused elsewhere. Colton and I studied together whenever we could; in person, on the computer, or on the phone.

I accepted our relationship for what it was: beautifully sweet. We were taking our time. It was based on more than sex, unlike other people we knew. Even if some of them were already doing more, it didn't matter to me. My high school memories didn't need to include that for me to be happy.

I did great on my finals.

Colton did, too, obviously.

He did *not* stay late at work the day of graduation. He was right there in the bleachers to accept his diploma. It was bittersweet to hug Quinn afterward. It was more so to be caught up in Sawyer's arms as he swung me around like a rag doll, his graduation gown trapping me in the blinding red of the material.

Colton did *not* punch Sawyer. He trusted him. And he would miss them, too. I was sure of it.

Just like they'd miss us.

It was such an achievement and I could not have been more proud when I got to see my boyfriend accept his diploma in front of so many people and he didn't have one of his 'moments'.

It felt like everything was finally coming together.

The start of something new for all of us.

* * *

Longer days bring longer nights and with it there's usually boredom. But not this time.

Amber L. Johnson

We were all so busy. It seemed like the months rushed by much faster than I could have imagined. Don't get me wrong, it was good. It just backed up that old saying that time flies when you're having fun.

Colton and I found a great little rhythm, and it seemed like he was less stressed without being in school. He was thriving at the museum, and focusing on his artwork, as well as spending time with our friends and me. But it was obvious our time alone was what he liked the most.

I had to agree.

When the weather would permit, we spent a lot of our time outside. Some of my best memories over the summer were of us in these secluded trees by the edge of a stream in the woods behind his house. A place where I could sit and read books while he painted.

Watching him paint in the open was beautiful. He seemed to capture the colors of nature so perfectly and it was almost magical to see him get lost in what he loved so much. By then, the silence between us was comfortable. We had all the time in the world, it seemed.

Those months made me appreciate a lot of things I had probably taken for granted for a long, long time.

John Lennon once said life is what happens when you're busy making other plans. He was pretty awesome and I get what he meant now.

I'm sure you're wondering why I've been writing about my relationship with Colton. Aside from the obvious hurdles we'd faced. Aside from the fact we're young. There has to be more to the story, right?

Sometimes change makes you sit up and pay attention, opening your eyes to so many new things, it's as if you'd been asleep for the first eighteen years of your life.

Plans change.

Life changes.

And as an after effect, love changes, too.

* * *

I helped plan his eighteenth birthday party with Sheila. Obviously, a surprise party wasn't going to work, so we made sure to have plans set in stone and told him well in advance and that it was a big deal for us to celebrate the fact he was amazing, alive, and in our lives.

Of course, it rained on his birthday and the plans we'd made had to be altered because we couldn't be outside for a barbecue in a downpour. His mom and I were clearly more

96

Puddle Jumping

disappointed than he was about things not going over as well
as we hoped. But all our friends were there and we kept the
amount of guests to a minimum so it could be intimate. So it
would *mean something*.

He seemed to genuinely have a good time, and Sheila
kissed me on the head as she was cleaning up while the last of
the guests were preparing to leave. She didn't need to say it
out loud, but it was obvious Colton hadn't had a birthday party
with friends in attendance *ever*. The fact we had to make a list
of who to invite in order to keep the numbers low made her
teary eyed.

I'll admit . . . it made me a little teary eyed, too.

After everyone left, the rain let up to almost nothing and
I asked Colton if he wanted to take a walk.

Honestly, I just wanted some alone time with him on his
birthday and I would take anything I could get. We set out
down the street, hand in hand, walking the sidewalk in silence
as the night turned darker. And it suddenly dawned on me
what his birthday meant in terms of our relationship.

"We're the same age, now." I laughed and held his hand
tighter.

"Did that bother you?" he asked, his head tilting in a
really cute way.

I shook my head. "No. I just like we're the same age
right now."

"Technically, you are still older than me by quite a few
months . . ." he started and I cut him off with a playful squeeze
to his shoulder.

"I don't care about technicalities. We're the same age.
Don't argue."

It had gotten easier over time. He was still very literal
and always would be, but if I stated my case well enough, he
would find the humor. We walked to the edge of the woods
and I leaned against an old tree that was huge, with thick
leaves dripping rain all down on the top of my head. But
watching Colton in the moonlight made any discomfort I had
seem so insignificant, that, at some point, I just stopped paying
attention to it all together.

I whispered into his ear I loved him and told him Happy
Birthday, promising him the next one would be even better.
And the one after that. I kissed him until I was sure the moon
was jealous.

Then, all at once, the moonlight disappeared and the
skies opened with a torrential downpour. Forget being upset

97

about the raindrops from the tree leaves. I was a drowned rat, laughing hysterically as buckets and buckets fell from the sky.

And as lightning flashed overhead followed by thunder so loud it made the ground beneath my feet shake, I caught a glimpse of that child-like wonder on Colton's face that he'd had all those years ago on the first day I went over to his house to pretend to babysit him.

This time he didn't cover his ears. Instead he grabbed my hand and started to run, jumping over puddles as we raced back to his house.

I love that memory.

Maybe the most.

* * *

Summer was almost over and I was so focused, had tunnel vision so badly, I must not have been paying attention. To any of it. Because now when I look back on it, there were little clues, I think.

I think there were.

Mrs. Neely called and asked me to invite my family over for a cook-out at their house. It was short notice, which was unexpected. But she was really excited about it, encouraging me to bring our friends as well. It didn't seem all out of the ordinary to invite them anymore. We just usually had more than a day's notice.

Either way, I showed up with my parents in tow. I'd barely had enough time to set my things down in the coat closet before being accosted by Harper and pulled away into the far corner of the backyard where the old swing set once stood.

Between her talking my ear off, and Mrs. Neely rushing back and forth between the backyard and the house, I didn't notice anything out of the ordinary.

I should have.

Contentment, you see . . . it causes blindness.

Later I would find out that Sheila let Colton make the decision to have all of us there for his big news. Unlike when he got the job at the museum and I found out through her, it had been arranged for her son to announce it himself. To everyone.

It was brand new. Less than twenty-four hours old.

The news that would rip a hole in my chest wide open and cause my entire life to fold in around me like a half-assed house of cards.

Puddle Jumping

He looked so *pleased*. And why not? It was quite an accomplishment, really. I couldn't argue. And he spoke directly to me when he said it out loud for the first time. Sheila gathered us around as she prompted Colton to speak. Her smile was so electric. She was proud. Beaming at how far he'd come. She stood by my side and squeezed my shoulders.

"He asked to tell everyone at once."

His father stood off with my parents, practically bursting with joy. My mom and dad were probably as confused as I was. And even though I was standing in a crowd of people I trusted and loved, I had never felt more alone than in that moment.

Colton, so happy and proud; smiling wide and eyes downcast for a moment before lifting, simply said it as best as he could.

"I've been offered an internship in England through the museum."

My heart died.

Fell right out of my chest and onto the bright green grass beneath my feet as I stared at him, muted by shock.

"I'll be boarding a plane to leave the country on August thirteenth at nine p.m." Another smile. Joyous applause and congratulations from the crowd of onlookers.

Except from me.

Except from me and my parents. Maybe Harper, too. I don't quite remember because the haze was too thick. The memory, while not that old, is hard to pinpoint because it's surreal, you know?

"The junior curator will accompany him. He'll be well taken care of." Sheila said it like it was the most obvious thing in the world and my heart wasn't breaking right beside her.

I dropped my cup at my feet; sticky liquid hitting my exposed toes. And I think that's when people started to get quiet.

"What about school?" My hands, they were shaking so badly, but I couldn't make them stop. We'd talked about this. I wasn't going far. We'd talked about transferring to the same college eventually. We'd talked about the future . . .

He looked at me with that expression that killed me on the inside. So honest. Pure. "I'll be tutored abroad."

It was then I lost all semblance of control, my head falling to my chest as I started to cry so hard I couldn't see. "You're leaving me?" Hands were on me. Comforting. My parents. Perhaps even Harper, but I wasn't sure because I didn't let it last too long.

Instead, I pushed by all of them, not even offering a final word to Colton as I ran through the backyard and into the house to escape out the front door.

chapter sixteen

I knew then. It was all over. There would be no way to be with Colton if we weren't actually together. The reality of how much our relationship depended on physical contact and constant close proximity crashed down on me like a ton of bricks as I stumbled down the driveway and onto the sidewalk. We had plans to go to school near each other so it wouldn't be an issue. We'd made *plans*.

I needed the time to think. To clear my mind. I could hear the voices of our respective mothers calling out for me. I could hear my father's voice above both of theirs. I knew the sound of the footsteps chasing after me were Harper's.

But they weren't the person I wanted to follow me across the street.

I wanted Colton.

And as of that moment, he was no longer mine. In just a few weeks' time, he would be in another country. Thriving, doing what he wanted to do more than anything else in his life.

Maybe our relationship had given him that confidence. He was going to go intern and paint in England. He would live this incredible life his parents had always dreamed of for him. He was going to be okay with this change to his routine because it involved his passion. His first love.

And I would be no one.

Just a girl with half her heart missing.

On some level, it was selfish of me to have left. But I couldn't see my actions beyond my tears. I walked until Harper pulled up in her car and demanded that I get in so that she could take me home. I packed my bags, left a note for my parents, and went to stay with her for the remainder of the weekend.

Harper raged. She hated Sheila. I should have been told aside from everyone else so I could properly respond. It was his mom's fault. But I knew better. Sure, she could see me as a girl in a relationship, but when it came down to it, she was a proud mother. And I had no idea if I would have responded in any other way if told one-on-one.

It didn't take the sting out of my reality, though.

I ended up sending Colton an email congratulating him on his opportunity. There was no way I could bring myself to talk with him. It was too painful to think he might have had a clue something was wrong, but not really . . . and the resulting conversations would be me lying the entire time to let him be happy-go-lucky about his future without me. I was selfish enough not to answer his because I couldn't bear to see what he would say.

My parents attempted to talk to me, but for once, I asked just to be left alone. And I guess they weren't used to that, so they did as I requested. There were a lot of phone calls involving yelling on my mother's end. I had to assume it was Sheila she was talking so harshly to. But I couldn't find it in myself to care.

I hadn't gone into a relationship with Colton to become dependent. I hadn't thought by integrating myself so thoroughly in his life, it would have resulted in me revolving my entire existence around him.

Such is first love, I suppose.

Everyone was worried. But I wasn't. I didn't care. If I could have faded into the walls, I would have.

A couple weeks before my birthday, my mom made me go see our family doctor. I didn't fight, even though I knew nothing was physically wrong with me. I was about to turn nineteen and instead of celebrating with my boyfriend; I had a tongue depressor in my mouth. My doctor's really cool and she ended up sitting down with me, asking what was going on. And when I described what had happened, in as little detail as possible, she looked sympathetic.

Not sympathetic enough to give me a Valium or anything

. . .

When I pulled up to my house and saw Sheila Neely's car outside, it made my insides nosedive straight through my floorboard.

It's funny how many scenarios went through my mind. One where I marched into the house and demanded she make Colton stay. One where I just drove and drove and drove until I ran out of gas and had to find a job waiting tables somewhere, like a character in a Nicholas Sparks book. One where I rammed my car through the front door and aimed straight for her kneecaps.

I guess I had some pent up aggression toward her I hadn't let myself acknowledge until that moment.

Puddle Jumping

But it seemed as good a time as any to get it off my chest. With more courage than I thought I possessed, I opened the front door to my house and what I saw in the living room shocked the hell out of me.

Sheila . . . face to face with my parents . . . holding a wrapped gift that was almost as tall as she was.

There was only one thing it could have been. Judging by the tears on her face and expressions on my parents', I knew Colton had painted me a gift.

And I knew he wasn't doing well. At all.

"What's going on?" I'd asked, suddenly hurting not just for me, but for the boy who had sent the gift.

"Colton wanted me to bring your gift over for your birthday. Since he will miss it."

My eyes barely met hers while I stared at the festive paper. "Why isn't he here to bring it?"

"He couldn't . . ." Her voice cracked and I just knew . . . he understood. He got it. The limited contact with me was wearing on him just as much.

I wanted to *yell* at her. I wanted to tell her all of the heartache could have been avoided, if things had just been handled differently. But I was as much to blame as she was, because I allowed my own feelings of self-pity to override what I knew Colton needed of me. He needed me to be supportive. He needed me to say congratulations and . . . just . . . *shit*, ya know?

I nodded and stepped forward, noting how my parents shifted protectively as I did.

"Do you mind if I talk to Lilly alone?" Sheila was breaking my heart with how genuine she sounded. But I knew what she and I had to discuss shouldn't have been overheard by my parents. I let them know it was fine and took a seat on the opposite couch, facing her as she settled back down, almost deflating right before my eyes.

"Do you not care about me?" It slipped out faster than I could stop it.

Her eyes got all big and she shook her head. "No. God, no. I can't believe you would think . . ."

"Then why didn't Colton tell me he was leaving? Or you, for that matter?"

Sheila held her breath for a moment before speaking. "In hind-sight, that is *exactly* what should have happened. We had no idea the internship even existed because . . . it didn't until he started there. They developed it specifically for him, and so as not to give false hope and take it away if it didn't pan out, they didn't mention it until it was final. Clearly, I would have liked to have known about it earlier, but I can't turn back the clock and do all of these things over again. I asked if he was going to tell you first. He was so proud, Lilly. He wanted it to be an announcement. He wanted you to be there along with everyone else. And you know once he has his mind set on something, it takes a crowbar to change it." Her brow furrowed. "When you showed back up in our lives at that craft fair, I was worried it would upset him. But after just a few minutes with you, he was calmer. He seemed so, at least."

"You didn't see me there." It was hard for me to believe what she was saying.

She laughed then. "I'm a mom. I see everything."

That was disturbing.

"I told you that I thought he had forgotten about you, even though I knew it would be virtually impossible for him to. From then on, he talked about you. Drew you. Painted you. I have an attic full of renderings of your face . . ." Her eyes went wide with panic. "I didn't want to upset you, so I never brought them down. But you were like the one point of light in a tunnel he could see so clearly. I guess, what I meant to say is, you've always been in his life. I'm shallow enough to have thought you always would be. Even after a year's worth of separation." There was a little smile of defeat. "You've been apart longer than that before. You're going away to college. It never occurred to me the distance would be an issue."

I saw her then. The real her. She was just human. Flawed. Sheila Neely was not a Super Parent. She was trying her hardest just like everyone else in the world. I'd put her up on such a pedestal that it was difficult to wrap my brain around the truth.

Searching for words wasn't easy. It took me a few minutes to get a steady train of thought before I could speak. "Has he been freaking out?" She nodded. "Breaking stuff. All of that?" Again with the nod. "I love him, you know. And not in a puppy love or teenage love sort of way. I know what it's like to be with someone because it's easy." I let that sentence sit for a moment. "Being with Colton is *not easy*. It's hard. It's work. But if I think about my life before him, and my life with him . . . the struggle and work is worth all of it."

She started to cry then. Like, really, really cry. But I couldn't comfort her.

"I promise that love isn't easy for anyone. Anywhere."

Puddle Jumping

"You're right. But if I had to choose between having what dumb people would refer to as a normal life and having a life with Colton, I would choose your son every single time." Without another word, I stood up and pulled the painting over to my feet, unwrapped it carefully, and let the paper fall away. "I would have boarded that plane with him, if given the chance. Spent my first year of college traveling and being there. I would have done all of it. If I had been given the chance."

Her silence was only punctuated by small sobs.

But I barely heard them.

Because I was staring at a painting *of* Colton. And he was staring back at me. His body situated in a way to convey sadness. His face solemn.

There, rounded in each corner, the colors overlapped his brush strokes that bore the words *I Love You* over and over and over . . . creating the backdrop of his heartbreak. And mine.

"Is he home?" I asked as I moved my feet, tripping over my shoelaces in my own haste.

"Yes."

She owed me time with him before he left. And she knew it. I watched her search for her keys in her pocket, but by the time she had them out for me, I was already at the door.

I didn't need them.

I had my own way in.

chapter
seventeen

I was worried about how he would react to me climbing through his window again after the weeks we'd had apart. One piece of me wondered if I would walk in on one of his meltdowns. Another piece wondered if he would be fine and Sheila had simply exaggerated to get me there.

On the way to his house, I called Harper and the conversation pretty much went like this.

"His mom came over . . ."

"I hate her."

"She didn't mean for it to happen. She asked him to tell me first."

"Hmm. Fine. I reserve the right to revisit my hatred at a later time."

"He painted me a picture of himself. It has *I Love You* written all over it."

"For real?"

"Yeah. I'm headed there now."

"Call me later."

I didn't even bother to park my car around the other side of the neighborhood. The sky was getting a little darker and I knew Mr. Neely worked mad, crazy hours. And even though I could have knocked on the door, I felt like I needed to climb up that lattice one last time.

I did, with my heart thundering in my ears and my hands shaking from the anxiety I was drowning in. But once I checked the latch and realized the window was still unlocked, tears filled my eyes and I had to take a breath before actually climbing through.

I wondered if he left it unlocked the entire time without thinking about it . . . or if he checked it every night to see if it was still unlocked, just in case I came over.

Either way . . . it made me feel awful.

I stumbled into the room blindly, hoping to God once more that I wouldn't break anything as I attempted to untangle my feet from the windowsill. When I righted myself, I realized

Puddle Jumping

the art room was pretty much vacant. Everything was put away. It felt wrong. Weird. I'd never seen it like that before.

Of course, Colton hadn't left me before, either.

After bracing myself for a moment, I walked slowly to the door and looked down the hallway toward his room, noting the soft tinkling of music filtering into the open space. I watched the lighting in his room shift, his shadow appearing and disappearing with his footsteps.

Back and forth.

Preparing to leave.

Or was he pacing?

No longer worried about my timing, I crept to his open door and stood there, watching him as he moved a foot and then back, his eyes downcast as his hands started to reach for something and then would stop and he would repeat the movement over and over again. He appeared to be so *very* frustrated.

I knocked gently on his wall, holding my breath as he turned abruptly and stared at my face. Just stared. No words.

"Hi," I called to him quietly.

His reaction surprised me. In the blink of an eye he rushed forward and wrapped his arms around my waist, pressing me to the wall and burying his face in my neck as he breathed in deeply and squeezed all the air from my lungs.

"Nothing works," he started, his hands kneading my sides as he tried again. "I try. And try. But nothing works. I can't focus. I can't . . . I can't."

"I'm sorry." I had to stop myself. "I apologize for not coming to see you sooner."

"You were upset. I hurt you. Something must have happened to make you stay away from me. Is that right?" His nose was pressed under my ear and I fought back another round of tears because he just didn't fully grasp it. He could have been repeating Sheila's words for all I knew.

"You're leaving."

His body went rigid, and slowly he pulled back from me to look down at his shoes. "You'd like it better if I stayed?"

"No!" It was a lie. But it wasn't. "This is . . . *such* . . . a great opportunity for you. You should go." His eyes met mine briefly. "But I'm going to miss you so very much while you're gone."

He nodded a little.

"Your mom delivered my birthday present. It's wonderful. Thank you."

A sad smile pressed his mouth upward. "I wanted you to have me with you."

The pain in my heart grew a thousand times over. "I know." My hand pressed to his cheek. "It was very thoughtful. Just like the words you painted . . ."

It was then his eyes met mine. I'm still not sure what he saw at that moment, but it felt like he was looking beyond my face and into my soul.

"I paint the truth, Lilly."

My heart stopped.

"I do . . . love you. If you needed me to say it before you should have told me so. I know what it means." The way he said it was like the words were forcing themselves from his mouth almost painfully, his face contorting as they left his lips and his eyebrows drew together. "This emptiness inside of me here," he placed my hand on his chest, "means I love you. When you're not here, I can't focus. It's too loud . . . But my heartbeat does this when you're close."

Under my palm, the erratic cadence was more apparent than I'd ever noticed before.

"I dream of you. And I don't like it when I can't talk to you or see you or touch you." His eyes found mine again. "That's love."

A sob broke through my chest as he pondered it. "Yeah, it is."

"Does my loving you make you sad?" Concern pulled at the corners of his eyes.

"No, I'm not sad you love me."

"Then why are you crying?"

I had to laugh a little, then. "Because I'm happy."

He was more confused. "Well, that doesn't make sense. Crying is for sadness."

"Sometimes," I laughed louder, "it means happiness. But . . . girls are strange."

His head tilted a little as he thought. "You would be more of an expert on that than I would be."

I pulled him closer, circling my arms around his waist and listening to his breathing while we stood, pressed against one another. I apologized, he accepted and we were fine, once again. It was the beauty of us. It was what it was. No games. No pretenses. No blame or guilt to deal with unnecessarily.

"Do you need me to help you finish packing?" I'd asked with my face smushed into the front of his gray t-shirt.

Puddle Jumping

"I'd prefer to kiss you for a while before you have to go home."

My smile started and then faltered. "I forgot to bring a toothbrush."

He was gone and back in less than five seconds, holding a brand new one in my face. "My mother bought an extra one for my trip."

Once again, I was thankful to Sheila for something.

He watched, as he always had, causing me to take a mental picture of him leaning against the wall as I spit and rinsed. And just as fast as I could get to him, I was in his arms.

The door was locked. The music was on. I mean, there weren't any candles or anything like that, but we were together one last time before he was going to leave for a year. Our recent absence from one another did nothing to slow our passion. It only made it more forceful. Our touches were heavy handed. Meaningful. Lingering. I wanted him to remember all of it.

I wasted no time taking off his shirt. There was no hesitance in his hands as we fumbled with my own.

It was hot needy kisses of the here and now.

It was: *take this with you when you leave.*

It was: *keep this in your memory when you lay in bed at night.*

It was: *You have all of me now.*

Our fingers explored one another. I was committing him to memory with my eyes closed and body erupting in goose bumps while becoming overheated at once. He studied my scar and his fingers trailed over the raised flesh again, so softly . . . I knew he remembered how he'd saved me once. But the truth was, he'd saved me again since then.

My touch was rough, just like he wanted. My kisses were insistent, just as they needed to be.

When I realized I was flat on my back on top of his bed, there wasn't a thought in my mind. I savored every touch. Every kiss. Each graze of my lips to his skin, willing my brain to just *remember*.

And when he pulled back off me, his lids half open and his hips dipping forward like before, I didn't stop him. I watched, fascinated.

Books and movies make it seem so much easier, like it just happens. But there's more to it. It just seemed to take a little longer than I had anticipated. I wasn't going to complain,

109

Amber L. Johnson

because in that moment I wanted to be with him in one last way.

If he was leaving, he was taking everything I had to give with him.

His forehead was creased with . . . worry? Pain? I couldn't tell because I was trying so hard not to cry over the finality of it all. I was too tense. It was too much.

It suddenly occurred to me he must have been experiencing that times a million.

"Colton, look at my face," I called to him and he did as I said, his eyes watching my lips as I spoke. "Relax . . ." As soon as I said it, I think we both loosened up at the same time, and it finally, finally happened.

It wasn't painful with Colton. He didn't rush the experience. It was so overwhelming for him that he was struggling to breathe. I shifted then, only minutely, to pull his face to mine with my hands, gripping the back of his neck tightly. Then I crossed my ankles behind his back. And squeezed my thighs against his torso.

Hard.

I believe we both had our eyes closed for just a moment, but I opened mine at one point to see him staring down at me in wonder, his mouth open as if he were struggling to speak.

But we didn't need to talk. We were communicating just fine.

A lot of girls probably lose their virginity and it's fast or painful, careless or upsetting.

Mine was not like that.

It was awkward and it did hurt a little. But I was with Colton. He was my first. My only. And it caused me to shake as his head fell to my shoulder and he pressed his lips to my neck.

"Lilly. Lilly." He just kept repeating it over and over.

I loosened my grip around his waist and I held onto him as he squeezed my side with one hand, using all the strength he had, pinning me to the mattress, making a breathless sound against my neck before it was over.

My shaky fingers touched his face, waiting for him to relax. I was afraid he would freak out. But as he pulled away from my neck, his eyes appeared serene. His fingertips traced over the side of my head and then lower across my ribcage until I could feel them on my hip.

Ever so gently brushing love against my skin.

* * *

110

Puddle Jumping

Afterward, I just held him, lying on his chest until he fell into a deep sleep. My ear stayed pressed to his sternum, listening as his breathing evened out and heartbeat slowed. Only a few tears escaped when I closed my eyes, caressing his side and across his chest with my fingers.

He'd said he loved me in more ways than one.

I whispered into the darkened room I would miss him more than he would ever understand. That I loved him more than my heart could take.

But I didn't allow myself to fall asleep. I couldn't justify wasting that precious time. A while later I heard his mom walk in the front door and I waited to see if she would come up to his room, but she never did. Maybe the silence in the house was enough for her to know things were all right.

With as much as it made me sick to my stomach, I forced myself off his chest and out of his bed. After one last look at his handsome face. Touching his chin with my fingertips. Watching his eyes move behind their lids

I kissed his nose. Once.

Before I could talk myself out of it, I dressed and left his house. Not looking back. I couldn't handle the thought of sleeping through the night and waking up to him saying goodbye. Or having him change his mind and staying because of me.

He needed to go.

It wasn't until I got behind the wheel of my car that the seriousness of what was occurring hit me so hard. I'd lost my virginity to the boy I loved. And he was leaving in less than twenty-four hours.

I cried the whole way home, allowing myself to *feel* what was happening and accepting it for what it was. There was no turning back. It was set in stone and the faster I mourned the loss and moved beyond that pain, the faster I could focus on other things.

* * *

I don't believe there's such a thing as conventional love. Love is bending. Love is breaking. Love is constantly learning about the other person until you go crazy because it will never be perfect, but there's no fault in trying.

I've loved a boy who was extraordinary beyond words, in my eyes.

I don't think I'd ever wanted to live an exceptional life before him. A life filled with color and knowledge and feeling beautiful.

111

But for a little while, I had it.

I suppose I thought maybe as much as I learned from him, he would have learned something from me, too. It's not easy. Not in any capacity. But I can't begin to wish it had never happened. I can't find it in myself to regret a single second we had together.

What I wanted was for him to see me and want me to be with him. What I wanted was for him to say he loved me – with words – and mean it. I needed these things that were out of my reach, and yet I continued to hold out hope.

And it happened.

He'd always be sweet and kind. He would always be the boy I had fought so hard for. But when there's separation involved, I couldn't be sure it would all stay the same. I worried about the change in his routine. That he wouldn't adapt to his new surroundings. I was thankful he had someone from the museum going with him, but I had to wonder if they knew him like I did. If they were going to take the time and effort to really learn and provide what he needed.

I wondered if he would miss me.

There's no shame in it, feeling sad and broken hearted over things I can't change. There's no magic formula. No time machine to go back. There's just what we've been handed and how we deal with it. I made mistakes when it came to a lot of things.

But no one, anywhere, could say I didn't give it my absolute best.

When I imagined Colton's face as he would be boarding his flight with his mentor, my heart broke all over again.

But there was nothing I could do about it. It was out of my hands.

I just wish I had started writing about it earlier while things were fresh in my mind, instead of with hindsight of what was to come. It makes it a little harder to be impartial.

I always wanted it to work out between us, but even if it doesn't, I guess I can say I'm grateful for the ability to have *met* someone like Colton, much less been able to love him as much as I do. I just have to keep telling myself that. Every day. All three hundred and sixty-five of them.

This could be where the story ends. And it hurts a million times over to think it could be true. That this is it.

Because, regardless of where my heart is going, my body is still here.

Puddle Jumping

It really is a shame more movies aren't like real life. Maybe then we wouldn't have such high expectations and feel let down by our own existence so much.

Who knows? Maybe someday I'll be his and he'll be mine. And space or time won't matter because we were meant to be.

But I won't hold my breath. Life doesn't usually work out the way we hope.

More than anything I want him to be happy. And maybe one day I will be, too.

epilogue

There was a time when I believed I wasn't going to fall in love. But I did.

This was followed by the thought that the boy I fell in love with could never love me back. But he does.

And he loves me in the very best way he knows how.

Four months passed while Colton was in England. My fears slowly dwindled the first time his face appeared over Skype. He didn't make much eye contact initially and his attention diverted from me to the things around him, especially if his mentor was watching the television too loudly.

But we learned.

He had to find his way on his own. Make friends. Adapt to change. I could tell, even in those brief moments I had with him that he was changing. It was hard for me, knowing I didn't have a part in it. But maybe, in some way, I did.

So we kept up the routine. Every Thursday at eight p.m. my Skype would ring. I made sure I was always in the dorm. And my roommate was out doing something else. She and I had an agreement.

"I miss you." I watched his face through the screen as he stared at mine.

"I'll be home in twenty-seven days."

I smiled. "I know. And I'm really happy about that."

"I'm glad you're happy." He grinned, like he meant it.

"Do you have anything you'd like to do when you get home?"

He nodded, his focus floating to the left of the screen. "I'd like to kiss you, if that's all right with you."

"I think that can be arranged."

* * *

College was stressful that first semester, but the little moments I could get with Colton made me feel less anxious. More grounded. I had papers and homework up to my ears, though I couldn't say that to the boy behind the screen.

I went out of my way to meet new people. Go to parties. Experience college. Never once did my friendship with Harper suffer. I didn't allow space between the new friends we'd made to alter the relationships we'd already had.

Friendship, as I'd once told my boyfriend, is important.

But I had space. I had time to find myself again.

The best thing about being apart was that I decided on my major. I focused on me. Set a goal that I would accomplish on my own.

I've had a lot of accomplishments in my life. I didn't die. I graduated high school. I got into the college of my choice.

But I would never call loving Colton an accomplishment. It was an honor. It changed me. It made me actually become the person I'd tried so hard to be all those years ago.

So I don't think it came as a surprise to anyone that being with my boyfriend had made me see things in a new light. I never would have known the type of person that I could be without having met him. If I had it in me to make a difference in one person's life, why not others? Maybe one day I'd teach my own PEERS class and some cute boy would lean against the wall in a hallway and tell the girl that loves him, 'Whatever'.

And I'd be there to see it happen.

The night I declared my major, ironically, was the first time he asked me about our situation.

"Do you wish I hadn't left you?"

"Of course. I miss you. I wish you were here every single day. But you're glad you went, right? Look at all you've accomplished."

"I wish you could have come with me."

"Me, too."

It was something we hadn't discussed before and my chest was hurting when we hung up.

I dreamed of him often and I worried about him constantly. And I thought, maybe when he came back home for Christmas, it would *not* be the same and the distance was too great for us to reconnect.

Maybe that would be the way a Hollywood movie about the subject would end.

But we're more than that.

When that day came, I stood right next to Sheila, holding her hand, and raising a yellow sign with my boyfriend's name on it while he departed the plane. I wasn't surprised he hugged his mom first. But it was only because once his arms were around me, he didn't let me go. Not through the airport. Not in the car. Just barely at his door to greet his dad.

115

Otherwise . . .

Nothing had changed. Not for the worse, anyway. No, in fact, it felt a hundred times better. Knowing what it was like to be apart made reconnecting so much sweeter.

He smelled the same. He felt the same. His eyes searched my face while he smiled and said my name over and over until I kissed him to quiet his whispers.

I stayed at his house and my parents didn't even mind. I was an adult and could make my own decisions, and as long as the Neely's didn't object, I was free to do so.

On Christmas morning I held Colton's hand while his parents stacked gifts all around us. Right before the unwrapping began, my parents showed up. I should have thought it was unusual, but it was Christmas morning, after all.

They settled by the fireplace and passed out their own presents, until we were surrounded by what felt like a wall of festive paper and shiny silver bows.

It didn't take long for us to get through every single box. Thank yous were exchanged, and just when I thought I'd be free to change out of my pajamas and take a shower, Mrs. Neely bent down in front of me and placed an envelope in my lap.

"What's this?" I had an inkling it was another pass to the museum, so I narrowed my eyes prepared to tell her I didn't really need them since her son had unlimited access to the exhibits. But just as I opened my mouth, my boyfriend cut me off.

"We asked your parents if it was okay."

I stared at his face, confused while I held the envelope in my hands and waved it at him. "There are museum passes in here, right?"

Mr. Neely leaned forward and I caught a glimpse of my mom as she covered her mouth and tears welled up in her eyes. My father took a deep breath and exhaled loudly.

Sheila reached out and ran her fingers across my cheek. "We want you to go."

My fingers trembled as I tore open the envelope and I lost my breath staring at the ticket in my hand.

"Really?"

It was Colton who answered, his voice steady and unwavering. "I want you there, Lilly."

I was blinded by tears. "Are you sure? Certain? Are you certain?"

Puddle Jumping

He didn't need me to go with him so I could be there to make sure he was okay. To ensure he kept his routine and didn't feel lonely.

He wanted me.

"I'm sure and I'm certain."

"The flight leaves on the third." Mom's voice was shaky and my dad reached for her hand.

My mind raced with every unanswered question and every promise of tomorrow. But when I looked at my boyfriend and how he was really, really smiling – that his eyes were finally looking at mine for longer than a second's worth of time – I knew.

Hollywood has to get their happy endings from somewhere. And even though the road is filled with bumps and bruises along the way, there's always the possibility of happiness in the end. I'm living proof.

My education won't be within the confines of a brick building while I sit in plastic chairs. Not anymore. Life is meant to be lived, and if you're offered the chance to experience exceptional things with an extraordinary person, then there isn't one reason in the world to say no.

And I didn't. I said yes because our love is no different than anyone else's. It's ours and that's all that matters.

It's a true story of a girl falling for a boy.

Nothing more.

Nothing less.

And I wouldn't want it any other way.

Amber L. Johnson

about the author

Amber is a full-time mom, full-time wife, is employed full time, and writes when she can. She believes in Happily Ever After's that occur every day - despite the obstacles that real life serves up on a regular basis. Or perhaps they're sweeter simply because of them. She always has two rubber bands on her wrist, a song in her head, and too much creamer in her coffee cup that reads 'Cocoa' - because she's a rebel. If she's not at her desk, with her boys, or behind the computer, she's supporting live music with her arms raised above her head and eyes closed, waiting for the drop.

Amber L. Johnson

acknowledgments

There are a million and one people to thank for this book seeing the light of day.

First, thank you to the immense amount of people that read the first draft. I hope you enjoy the revisions and that it still holds a place in your heart.

Lori Wilt, you make me accountable for every word, and I thank you for being one of my most trusted sets of eyes. Immense gratitude to you and FicWishes for always supporting every single one of my endeavors.

Stephanie Alexander, thanks for telling me to tone it down, even when I didn't want to. I'll return the favor every single time.

Kathie Spitz, you never touched the original but your fingerprints are all over this one. Twice. I thank you for telling me not to give up because I actually listened this time.

April Brumley, you are an inspiration in more ways than I can count. Thanks for letting me use your brain when mine has gone to mush. You always look with your special eyes and see the things I can't.

To the countless women, parents, professionals and wonderful people who allowed me to speak to you in multiple capacities – you helped make this decision easier and gave me more hope than you'll ever know.

Angela V., Amber S., Kristy H., Marty K., Alex O. Aislyn D. and Stephanie R. – thank you all for pre-reading and giving feedback that made this better than it would have been without it. You're book-stars.

Mary Elizabeth, your support has been more than I could have hoped for. Try not to forget the little people when you're at the top of the NYT, yeah?

Shannon, I hope you know how much your professional opinion means to me. It may not be perfect, but we know there's no such thing. Thanks for being a bright spot in a cloudy sky.

Jayne Compton, thank you for those words of encouragement all those years ago. Your PEERS –type class and their responses to this story changed my life in the greatest way.

Finally, Alec Frazier, your feedback, phone calls and open discussions on life with Autism have made an incredible impact on me. I'll be eternally grateful for your endorsement, your reactions and most importantly the hope you give me for my son's future.

endorsed by

To learn more about Alec Frazier's story, and Autistic Reality, an autistic-run advocacy and public relations firm, please visit his website at: http://www.nothingaboutuswithoutus.net/

For up to date information, "Like" the Autistic Reality Facebook Page at: https://www.facebook.com/autisticreality

Made in the USA
Lexington, KY
08 July 2014